# ONCE UPON A COWBOY

RACHEL LACEY

Once Upon a Cowboy
Copyright © 2019 by Rachel Lacey
Ebook ISBN: 9781641970907
POD ISBN: 9781074807887

Cover Design © Letitia Hasser, Romantic Book Affairs

NYLA Publishing
121 W 27th St., Suite 1201, New York, NY 10001
http://www.nyliterary.com

# ONCE UPON A COWBOY

## 1

———

*M*egan Perl slipped through Rosemont Castle's front doors as sunrise brightened the sky outside, brand new Canon digital camera in her hands. Her breath fogged the air in front of her as she jogged down the steps, tucking her chin into the fold of her scarf as she went. She crossed the circular drive out front before turning to face the castle.

Gingerly, she lifted the camera out of its case and turned it on, adjusting the shutter to capture the sun as it crept up behind the castle, making its stone façade seem to glow. *Beautiful.* Sometimes she still couldn't believe this place existed, tucked into the Appalachian Mountains here in Towering Pines, Virginia, or that she and her two best friends were lucky enough to work here.

Megan crouched down, looking up at the castle through the camera's lens. She snapped a series of photos as the sun rose over the tower on its left-hand side, capturing the way the light reflected in the castle's many windows as it rose higher in the sky. These were the details she'd always loved to photograph most.

From behind her, the sound of a diesel engine rumbling up

the drive disturbed the otherwise quiet morning. She turned, watching as a shiny black pick-up truck pulled up in front of the castle and parked. This must be Jake Reardon, the man who had recently rented the stable and farmhouse on the grounds. He was supposed to be moving in today, although she hadn't met him yet. She didn't know much about him except that he was a widower and well-liked around town. And apparently, he liked to get a *really* early start on moving day.

The door to the cab opened, and the man inside stepped out, turning to face her. She took in his lean, muscular frame, the well-fitted jeans and brown leather boots.

*Well, hello there...*

A fluttery sense of awareness filled her belly as her gaze swept up to meet his, warm brown eyes set in a handsome—if solemn—face. But, wait. She'd stared into those eyes before. She knew this guy. Well, she didn't know him, exactly, but for a few memorable seconds across a bar last summer, they'd shared a definite...moment.

She swallowed over the dryness in her throat. "Are you Jake Reardon?"

He nodded. "I am."

"Megan Perl." She extended her hand. "We must not have been formally introduced that night at Bar None. When I heard you were moving onto the property, I didn't realize we'd already met."

"I hadn't put two and two together either." His voice was deep and rich. It had captivated her that night last summer, and it had the same effect on this chilly spring morning. His gaze was steady yet intense, locked on her face.

Instinctively, she dipped her head so that her hair fell across her left cheek, hiding the scars marring her skin. "Well, this is a happy coincidence."

"It sure is." Jake was seemingly unaffected by her appearance. He didn't flinch or look away, as some other men had, but there was no heat in his gaze either. That night at Bar None, the air between them had sizzled with attraction. The absence of it from him now was enough to douse the spark still simmering in her belly. Maybe he wasn't interested anymore. Maybe he'd found someone else in the months since, or maybe he no longer found her attractive.

She cleared her throat. "I have to confess, I didn't expect to see you until later today. Getting an early start?"

"I just stopped by to get the keys, so I can get the barn prepped before I bring my horse over this afternoon."

"Oh, okay. I can get those for you." She tucked her camera inside its case.

"Are you a photographer?" he asked, stepping closer.

She nodded. "Still something of an amateur."

"Can I see?" He gestured to the camera.

A warm flush spread over her skin as she pulled the camera back out, turned on the display screen, and showed him one of the shots she'd just taken. The sun's rays burst from behind the tower like a halo, just as she'd envisioned.

"Wow. I'm impressed," he said, his tone sincere. "That doesn't look like an amateur shot to me."

"I've never had any formal training, but I've taken some online classes," she said with a shrug, uncomfortable with his praise. "And lots of practice."

"We learn by doing," he agreed. "That's how I became a horse trainer."

"Really?"

"Took a job mucking stalls at a barn near me when I was a teenager to help pay the bills. Before I knew it, I was spending all my free time there, helping out wherever I could. Turns out, I'm good with horses. Who knew?" He offered a self-deprecating smile.

"I'll, um, I'll get those keys for you," she said, motioning for him to follow her up the steps into the castle. She led the way into the office, where she pulled out a large white envelope that contained the keys to the barn and farmhouse. She and Jake sat down and went over the remaining paperwork before she handed him the envelope.

"Look forward to moving in," he said as he stood, those brown eyes sizzling into hers.

"We're looking forward to having you here," she said. "And I personally can't wait to see horses grazing out there on our pastures."

"Guess I'll see you around, then." He extended his hand, and she took it. His grip was firm and warm, and it sent a ripple of heat up her arm like she'd just slipped her hand into a hot bath.

"Just let us know if you need anything." She pressed her hand—the warm one—against her chest as he walked away. Okay, she seriously needed to get her hormones under control now that Jake was going to be living and working here on the property.

She picked up her camera and headed upstairs to her room. She and her friends Elle and Ruby had won a contest last year that had led to permanent positions as Rosemont Castle's property managers. Since their arrival, they had opened an inn inside the castle, as well as instituting other programs that helped the property pay for its own upkeep.

As she walked down the hall toward her bedroom, she passed Ruby coming out of the spiral stairwell that led to her bedroom at the top of the tower. "Good morning."

"Morning," Megan said with a smile. "I just met our new tenant and gave him his keys."

"Oh, wow. He's here early."

"Right?" Megan said. "Hey, did you know Jake was the guy we met at Bar None that night last summer when we bumped into Theo and his friends there?"

Theo was Theo Langdon, Rosemont Castle's owner and also the Earl of Highcastle, who—after falling in love with Elle —had chosen to live here in Virginia in the castle his grandfather built rather than returning to his home in London.

"Of course," Ruby said. "You didn't?"

"No," Megan said, trying not to sound annoyed. "Do you need my help with breakfast this morning?"

"Nope," Ruby told her. "Elle and I have it covered. Enjoy your morning off."

"Thanks."

With a wave, Ruby headed downstairs, while Megan went into her bedroom to get her two foster dogs—already bouncing excitedly as they caught sight of her—out of their crates. Chandler was a fluffy black dog, a mix of who-knew-what, but one hundred percent happy energy. Barnaby was as quiet as Chandler was exuberant, a tan-colored pit mix who preferred to let Chandler do all the "talking" for him.

Megan let them out of their crates and sat on the bed. She pulled her camera out of its case and started tabbing through the photos she'd taken outside while the dogs chased each other around her room. The pictures were...not bad. Pretty good, even? Okay, there were a few shots here she couldn't quite believe she'd taken herself.

Photography had always been a hobby, but she'd saved enough money during her first year here at the castle to buy this fancy new camera, and now she wanted to make it more than a hobby. She'd been toying with the idea of offering portrait sessions to their guests at the castle, but so far, she hadn't worked up the courage to ask Ruby and Elle what they thought of the idea.

Maybe she hadn't felt "professional" enough to charge money for her photos. But Jake's words resonated with her. *We learn by doing.* He'd learned his trade by trial and error the same way she was, and now he'd moved here to start his own horse training business. Maybe it wasn't so crazy for her to charge for her services either. Maybe she'd run it past her friends tonight.

She pulled out her laptop and spent the next hour or so editing a few of the best shots she'd taken that morning. They would make a great addition to her portfolio, not to mention the castle's online photo gallery. Finally, she stood and went into the bathroom to get ready for her day, blanching when she caught sight of herself in the mirror.

She'd been in such a hurry to photograph the sunrise, she hadn't done her makeup yet, which meant...Jake had seen her bare face. Without the special concealer she applied every morning, the left side of her face was marred by a thick, pink scar that started near her scalp and ran down her cheek, jagged in areas where the tree branch had ripped haphazardly through her skin during the crash. Another scar extended from her left shoulder to her elbow.

She closed her eyes, swallowing over the tightness in her throat. It didn't matter. She wasn't interested in dating him anyway. She had already decided she was focusing on her photography this year. No men. Only here, in the privacy of her bathroom, with tears burning in her eyes, could she admit —just to herself—she wasn't ready to date. Not yet.

And anyway, she'd already spent too many years indulging in meaningless hookups, flitting from one dead-end job to another, and putting herself last. This year was all about Megan and no one else. She had a chance here at Rosemont Castle to explore what really made her happy, to maybe discover a more mature version of herself.

She carefully applied her makeup. Then—armor in place— she leashed her dogs and walked them outside. "Any day now, Mother Nature," she grumbled as she led Chandler and Barnaby over the dewy grass alongside one of the pastures. Her breath glistened in front of her as frosty evidence of every exhale. After almost a year in the mountains of Virginia, she still hadn't acclimated to the weather. Maybe she'd always be a Florida girl at heart.

From inside her jacket, her cell phone began to ring. She fished it out clumsily with her gloved fingers and connected the call. "Hello."

"Hi, Megan, it's Priya." Priya was their contact at the

Towering Pines Animal Shelter. She helped them coordinate everything with the rescue pets they were fostering here at the castle in their Fairy Tails program.

"Oh hey, Priya, how are you?" Megan juggled both leashes in her right hand as she held the phone in her left.

"Great, thanks. I'm calling with a rather unusual question."

"Okay," Megan said, intrigued.

"A few weeks ago, the local humane society seized three neglected horses, which have been under quarantine at their livestock rescue facility. But this morning, they were made aware of a hoarding situation that's going to require all their resources, and long story short, they need to move those original three horses somewhere until they're adopted."

"Foster homes for horses?" Megan turned her gaze toward the barn just visible ahead, realizing where Priya was going with this.

"Yes. These horses will still be under the care of the humane society, but since their facility is full, they reached out to us to see if we might have any foster homes that would be able to accommodate them." She paused. "Which is why I'm calling, since, as I recall, you have an empty barn and pastures. I could probably find someone to come out and help care for them if you could take them in, even temporarily."

Megan grimaced. She really did want to help, but... "I hate to tell you this, but we've rented out the barn. In fact, our new tenant is moving in today. I'm not sure how many horses he's bringing with him, though. I could ask him if he's got room for the foster horses."

"Oh, could you? That would be great. Sheriff Alvarez has room for one of them at his house, so I'd just need you to take two."

"You mentioned they were under quarantine?" Megan asked.

"It's standard with livestock to make sure they aren't

carrying infectious diseases, but these horses were given the all clear a few days ago. They're ready to move," Priya told her.

"Okay. I'll ask our new tenant. I can probably let you know later today." She looked down at the barn, but Jake's black truck was nowhere to be seen. So, he'd already left to get his horse.

"Perfect. The humane society needs to act quickly on this hoarding situation, so the sooner the better."

"Got it," Megan told her, turning around to head back toward the castle.

"Out of curiosity, who rented the stable?" Priya asked.

"Jake Reardon."

"Oh really?" Priya's tone changed, and Megan had the sudden impression she might not be the only one who found her new tenant handsome.

"Yep. He's starting his own horse training business."

"That's great. Good for him. Well, let me know what he says. I'd love to get the horses moved as soon as this afternoon if he's amenable."

Megan pressed a hand against her heart, which was beating just a little bit faster at the idea of seeing Jake again so soon. "Okay. I'll ask him as soon as he gets here."

JAKE REARDON WALKED to the end of the barn and stood looking out over the empty pastures beyond. Moving into the farmhouse at Rosemont Castle was the fresh start he'd been depending on for years now, the chance to step into his own shoes for the first time as he grew his business. It had been a hell of a road to get here, but he wasn't going to think about that right now.

Focus on the positive. And, speaking of positive, Megan Perl was currently walking toward him from the direction of the castle. Megan, the woman who'd stolen his breath that night at Bar None last year, who made him feel alive for the

8

first time in recent memory, and who also managed the property he'd just leased.

"Hi," she said as she approached the barn. "Settling in okay?"

"Well, my horse is," he told her. "I haven't even been over to the house yet."

"Busy day for you." She tucked a strand of glossy brown hair behind her ear as she came to stand beside him in the entrance to the barn.

"It sure is."

"Can I meet your horse?" she asked with a smile.

"Of course." He led the way into the barn. Twister hung his chestnut head over his stall door, whinnying to them as they approached. "This is Twister," Jake said as the horse headbutted him affectionately. "Bet you can't tell how he got his nickname."

Megan reached out to touch Twister's face, running her hand over his tornado-shaped white blaze. Her smile widened. "Clever."

Twister paced to the window at the rear of his stall and whinnied again before returning to the doorway.

"He's a little lonely this afternoon," Jake said. "I don't think he likes being the only horse on the property, but he won't be for long. A client is dropping off a horse for me to train later this week, and I'm hoping to make that two by the end of the month. I'll rent out the rest of the stalls to boarders."

"That's actually what I came down here to talk to you about," she said. "Are you familiar with the program we're running at Rosemont Castle?"

"Only what I've heard around town," he told her.

"Well, when Elle, Ruby, and I came in as property managers last year, we opened an inn inside the castle, so guests can come and have a 'royal' getaway. There are twelve guest rooms that were sitting empty, and now they're generating income for Theo and his family to help Rosemont Castle pay for its own keep, so to speak."

"Sounds good," he said, not having any idea what this had to do with him.

"We also run a program with rescue pets. It's called the Fairy Tails program," she said with another of those irresistible smiles. "Get it? T-a-i-l-s."

"I like it," he said, returning her smile.

"We foster adoptable dogs and cats from the Towering Pines Animal Shelter here at the castle, and our guests can meet them while they're here. Then, if they're interested in adopting, they can put in an application and hopefully take their new pet home with them when they leave. It's been really successful so far, and popular with our guests."

"That's great." He stared at her, momentarily distracted by the way the sun danced in the cinnamon depths of her eyes. Megan seemed to radiate energy, making everything feel lighter and brighter when she was nearby. It was more than just physical attraction—although he certainly felt plenty of that too. He'd felt a sort of instant connection with her that night at Bar None, and the intervening months had done nothing to dampen his interest.

Whatever was or wasn't between them, though, he couldn't afford to become distracted by it. He and Megan were linked by business now that he lived here at Rosemont Castle, and that meant she was off-limits romantically, assuming he was even ready to embark on his first relationship since Alana's death, and he wasn't at all sure that he was.

"Anyway, I got a call from the Towering Pines Animal Shelter this morning," Megan told him. "They're trying to help the local humane society place some rescued horses and were wondering if we could put them up here in the barn until they find homes."

Jake rocked back on his heels, frowning. As much as he wanted to say yes, he needed to rent out these stalls to keep himself afloat. His new business was barely off the ground, and right now, his budget was stretched as thin as the prickly whiskers on Twister's chin. "What do you know about their background?"

"Only that they were seized due to neglect. Priya said they'd completed a quarantine period and were ready to move. The humane society needs to clear out their livestock facility to make room for animals they're seizing from a hoarding situation."

"And who would care for them?" he asked.

"She said she might be able to send someone out to help. And the humane society would pay any expenses like feed and medical care."

"Hmm." He watched as Twister began to nibble at the hay in his stall. Neglected horses would require a lot of extra care, even if the humane society sent someone out to help.

"I hate even having to ask, and I totally understand if you say no," Megan said. "It's the worst timing, right? If only they'd needed a place to put a couple of foster horses anytime over the last year, we would've been able to take them in a heartbeat."

"Although you wouldn't have had anyone to care for them," he commented, gut desire to help warring with the knowledge that doing so would put his new business at financial risk. And he'd already risked so much just to get this far.

"Very true," Megan said. "I wish I could give you some time to think about it, but apparently these horses need to be moved today."

"Any idea how quickly horses like that usually get placed permanently?" he asked, running numbers in his head. He might be able to get by without boarder income for a few months, depending on how many hours of business his off-site training clients generated for him.

"No," Megan said apologetically. "I could call Priya and find out, though. Our dogs and cats are usually with us anywhere from a few weeks to a few months, so I'd imagine horses would be similar."

"Priya Sharma?" he asked. They'd gone to high school together. Of course, he could say that about half the town, if they were anywhere near his age. He knew Priya better than most, though. She and Alana had been good friends.

As Megan nodded, a shaft of sunlight from the window in Twister's stall caught the scar that ran down the left side of her face. "She mentioned that she knew you too."

He'd heard peripherally about the car accident when it happened last year, although he hadn't realized at the time that he knew her. "It's not that I don't want to help, but these horses are likely to need a fair amount of time and attention to get them ready for adoption, and I really was counting on boarder income."

"I understand."

He rubbed Twister's neck as he realized the inevitability of what he was about to say. "But, far be it for me to turn away an animal in need, so I'll make it work."

Megan's expression brightened. "I realize this is a huge imposition, and we're more than happy to make it up to you any way we can."

An image of her in front of the castle that morning with her camera drifted through his mind. "Actually, maybe there is something you could do for me."

She nodded. "Just let me know what you were planning to charge to board two horses, and I'll subtract it from your rent until they're adopted. I already cleared it with Theo. We'll even throw in a little extra to account for the inconvenience."

"Oh." He straightened. "Well, I hate to…I mean…"

She waved away his pride. "Consider it done." Her eyes narrowed. "But wait…what were you going to ask me for?"

"It's nothing." He shook his head, embarrassed to put his idea into words, especially now that she'd offered financial compensation for the rescue horses.

She crossed her arms over her chest, giving him an amused smile. "Just tell me."

His cheeks felt too warm. "Well, I was going to ask if you could take some pictures for me, you know, while I'm working with the horses. For my website."

Her smile was wide and genuine. "I'd love to."

"No need. Really. Compensation for boarding is more than enough."

She placed a hand on his forearm. Her touch was light, casual, but it sent a burst of fire through his veins. "You're doing the humane society a huge favor by taking in these horses, and anyway, I'm building my portfolio right now, so I'd be getting as much out of it as you are."

"Well, okay then. I'd really appreciate it."

"It would be my pleasure." She was still smiling at him, and it was doing all kinds of uncomfortable things to his body, reminding him exactly how long it had been since a woman smiled at him with anything other than pity, or even touched his damn arm, for that matter. Let alone how long it had been since a woman had touched any other part of him. Maybe that was the reason he was about to lose his damn mind every time Megan so much as blinked in his direction.

"Okay, I'll leave you to get settled in, but I'll call once I've talked to Priya," she told him. "And thanks again. We really appreciate it."

"Don't mention it." He watched as she walked toward the castle, trying not to stare at the sway of her ass inside her jeans. Megan was tall and lean, curved in all the right places. Her mahogany hair shone in the sunlight. Gorgeous. Every inch of her. Megan's tanned complexion and dark hair and eyes were the opposite of Alana's pale features. He'd thought blonde hair and blue eyes were his "type," but lately, it was Megan's face inspiring his fantasies.

And he had a serious problem on his hands. He and Alana had started dating at fifteen. She'd been his first date, first kiss, first girlfriend, and he had been hers. But her strictly religious family had insisted she wait for her wedding night. After watching his mother's life disintegrate from too many men and drugs, Jake had been happy to wait if it meant being a part of the wonderful thing he'd shared with Alana, the glimpses of stability and happiness he experienced when he visited her parents' house.

And so, at just eighteen years old, he had walked down the aisle, ready to start his new life with the woman he loved. When he first heard the screams, when he saw Alana on the ground in her white dress, he'd thought she would jump up at any moment, laughing at her own clumsiness. It would be a funny story to tell. "Remember how you fell down the steps behind the VFW hall during our wedding reception?"

But Alana hadn't gotten up, laughing or otherwise. She'd gone into a coma, where she lingered for almost nine years. He'd been forced to watch her wither away in that hospital bed, becoming a fragile shell of the vibrant woman he'd loved since he was fifteen, until finally, she'd left him forever.

Now, Jake found himself in the most uncomfortable and unwanted position of being a twenty-eight-year-old virgin widower, and he had no idea what to do about it. Part of him wanted to get drunk at the local bar, take a woman home, and be done with it. But he couldn't do that in a small town like Towering Pines, not unless he wanted the whole town to know about it, anyway.

His attraction to Megan was quickly becoming a problem, though. There was no way he was going to lose his virginity with the woman who managed the property he'd just leased. That was asking for disaster. Megan was off-limits. If only he could as easily convince his body as his mind.

## 2

_____

The trailer rumbled up the drive just past five o'clock, and Megan hurried the rest of the way down to the barn to meet it. Jake was already waiting, hands shoved into the pockets of his well-worn jeans. Her gaze dipped to the way the denim hugged his lean muscular legs and cupped his firm ass. Quickly, she yanked her eyes up to his face before he caught her staring, but his gaze was locked on the trailer crunching over the gravel lot in front of the barn. For a moment, she got caught up in the equally distracting sight of his handsome face, coated now with a day's worth of stubble.

The truck's engine shut off, and Megan turned her attention toward the people climbing out of the cab. Priya was in the passenger seat. Megan didn't recognize the man who got out of the driver's seat, but Priya had told her Sheriff Alvarez would be transporting the horses tonight.

"Hi guys," Priya said as she walked around to the back of the trailer, long black hair blowing in the breeze. "Thanks so much for helping out with these horses. We would have really been in a bind if you hadn't had room for them."

"Happy to help," Jake said.

The sheriff walked toward them, extending a hand to

Megan. "Jesse Alvarez."

"Megan Perl," she said as she shook. "Nice to meet you."

He nodded, a friendly smile on his face. "Always nice to meet a new face in town. I've heard a lot about you and your friends since you came to Rosemont Castle. The whole town's buzzing about it."

She smiled, ducking her head. No doubt he'd also heard about the accident. The whole town had been buzzing about that too. "Thanks."

Jesse and Jake exchanged greetings, and then they opened the trailer, revealing the two horses inside—or their rear ends anyway. They were tethered facing away from the door with a partition between them. One horse was a tan color with a black tail, and the other had a white coat speckled with darker spots. Both of them shifted anxiously inside the trailer.

"They've already received veterinary care and completed a two-week quarantine," Priya told them. "They've had their Coggins and been dewormed. Someone from the humane society will be in touch tomorrow to schedule follow-up care for them."

Jesse stepped up and backed the black and brown horse off the trailer. "This is Dusty Star. Buckskin mare, approximately ten years old. Should be in good shape once she gets some weight on her."

Megan's gaze drifted to the way the horse's ribs protruded beneath her scruffy coat. Jake stepped forward to touch Dusty Star, running a hand down her neck in an affectionate way that seemed to help put the horse at ease. He and Jesse took her into the barn and settled her into a stall before returning for the second horse.

"They call this one Bug," Jesse said as he led the speckled horse off the trailer. "She's just a filly, about three years old. Quarter horse, but obviously part Appaloosa with her coloring. She was attacked by a pack of feral dogs and left to heal without medical attention."

Megan resisted the urge to flinch when she saw the wounds on the horse's face and neck, stained purple by whatever the humane society's vet had treated her with. The color stood out in sharp contrast against her white coat, giving her a slightly cartoonish look.

"She'll have some battle scars once she heals, won't you, Bug?" Jesse said, patting the horse's shoulder. Bug flicked her ears, dancing nervously to the side as they neared the barn.

*Scars.* Megan's chest felt like one of the horses was standing on it. The left side of her face ached the way it had in those first days after the accident, when the pain had kept her from thinking farther into the future than an end to the ceaseless throbbing.

As Jake and Priya followed Jesse and Bug into the barn, Megan turned and walked off into the gathering dusk, letting the shadows swallow her whole.

JAKE RELEASED A DEEP SIGH. It had taken over an hour to get the horses settled and all the paperwork signed for the foster arrangement with the humane society. Now, it was almost seven, and his stomach was impatiently reminding him he'd missed lunch in the chaos of the day. The sheriff's truck crunched down the lane away from the barn, tail lights gleaming in the dark.

Megan lingered in the doorway, eyes fixed somewhere in the distance. She'd been unusually quiet since the horses arrived, and she'd messed with her hair so that it covered the scar on her face. That made his gut churn with something other than hunger, something that made him want to brush her hair back and kiss every gorgeous inch of her skin until she saw herself the way he did, which was absolutely perfect.

"Long day," he said instead, mostly to break the silence that had fallen between them.

She turned toward him. "You must be exhausted. You just moved in a few hours ago, and here I am, pushing foster horses at you."

"The timing isn't great, but I'm glad we were able to help out." He looked in at Bug, contentedly munching hay in her stall. "Plus, I think Twister's glad for the company tonight."

Megan walked over to stand beside him, and they watched the horse in silence for a minute. "I'll never understand how someone could keep horses like this. How do you look at them and not feed them?"

"Humans are capable of unfathomable acts of cruelty," he said.

"We're the worst, aren't we?" She sounded almost surprised, hands resting lightly on the bars at the front of Bug's stall.

"I'd argue we're both the best and the worst of the animal kingdom."

"Hard to be both," she said.

"And yet, we manage it."

"Do you ever just…" She paused, staring at Bug's withered frame, dotted here and there with bite wounds. "Just look at something like this and fear for humanity?"

"Nah. Because, for every person who'd mistreat an animal, there are ten out there working to make it right and do good in the world."

"I hope so."

"Hey." He rested a hand on her shoulder. "You okay?"

She drew back, arms clasped across her chest. "What? Of course. Why wouldn't I be?"

"You tell me." He gave her shoulder a gentle squeeze.

"I'm okay," she said, but her voice had dropped a little, and this time her words sounded honest instead of defensive. "I guess seeing her like that just got to me a little bit."

"Yeah, me too. I don't see a lot of this kind of thing first hand. You guys are doing a great thing with your Fairy Tails program."

She gave him a small smile, fingers going absent-mindedly to her face to tuck her hair into place, no longer hiding behind it. "Did you manage to get yourself moved into the farmhouse earlier?"

"Well, my stuff's inside, and my bed's made. Beyond that, I'm not so sure, but that's a job for tomorrow."

She gave him a sympathetic look. "We really owe you one for spending your evening here at the barn instead of unpacking. Do you have anything for supper?"

At just the mention of food, his stomach grumbled loudly. He rubbed a hand against it. "I'm sure I can rustle something up." Although, the truth was, he knew for a fact his pantry was bare. Grocery shopping was another task for tomorrow.

"Come up to the castle and have dinner with us," she said.

"Thank you, but I don't want to intrude."

"Oh, come on." Laughter danced in her eyes. "I know you haven't had a chance to go grocery shopping yet. Come up and eat with us. Beatrice, our weekday chef, always fixes plenty. The least we can do is feed you after hijacking your evening."

"I don't know." He felt intensely uncomfortable with the idea of dining up at the castle. He was tired and sweaty from a day of moving and probably smelled like horses. He'd always been the help, never the guest. But then again, Megan was an employee at the castle too.

"I insist," she said. "We usually sit at the farm table in the kitchen. Nothing fancy."

"All right," he agreed reluctantly. "Thank you. Just let me go back to the house and clean up."

"Okay, come on up whenever you're ready. Theo's in town this week, so he'll probably be joining us too." She touched his shoulder as she walked away.

As Jake stepped into the shower five minutes later, he could still feel the warmth of her fingers as though she'd branded his skin.

By the time Megan made it into the kitchen, Elle and Ruby already had a bottle of wine open and were sitting at the bar top, chatting with Beatrice.

"How did it go with the foster horses?" Elle asked.

"They're here and settled, but they're in really bad shape, you guys. It kind of broke my heart." Megan slid onto the barstool beside Elle, grateful for the company of her two best friends after a long day. She, Ruby, and Elle had known each other since elementary school. Getting to live and work together here at Rosemont Castle was a dream come true for all of them, and they'd never been closer.

"I'll take a walk down and meet the horses in the morning," Ruby said. "I wanted to re-introduce myself to Jake too."

"Actually, you can do that tonight. I invited him to join us for dinner." Megan poured herself a glass of wine and took a grateful sip. "Theo's coming too, right?"

"Yep," Elle confirmed. "He'll be here any minute."

Beatrice set a basket of fresh rolls on the counter in front of them. "You have no idea how happy it makes me to see all of you guys around the dinner table every night. It was too quiet here for far too long."

Heavy footfalls echoed down the hallway, and Jake appeared in the doorway to the kitchen wearing a crisp black T-shirt and jeans, his hair still damp from the shower. Megan's whole body seemed to hum at the sight of him, like she and Jake were opposite ends of a magnet. This attraction wasn't going to be as easy to shake as she'd hoped.

"Hi," he said, something almost timid in his tone.

"Come on in," she said, waving him into the kitchen. "Jake, you may remember Elle." She gestured to the blonde beside her. "And Ruby." Ruby waved from the other end of the counter. "They were with me that night we met in Bar None. And this is Beatrice, the weekday chef here at the castle."

Megan indicated the older woman on the other side of the kitchen. "She's nothing short of amazing."

"No less amazing than these ladies here," Beatrice said with a warm smile. "Welcome, Jake. We're so glad to have you and to see those pastures filled with horses again." The barn and pastures had sat empty for over twenty years, when the Langdon family sold the last of their horses. Theo's grandmother—and the castle's namesake—Rose had been the true horse lover in the family, and after her untimely death, the barn had eventually fallen to disuse.

"Thank you," Jake said. "I'm glad to be here."

"There's beer in the fridge," Beatrice told him with a wink. "I always keep it stocked for Mr. Langdon."

"Did I hear my name?" Theo asked as he came into the kitchen.

Conversation flowed as freely as the wine while their group settled around the table for dinner. Theo, Elle, and Ruby sat on one side of the table, with Megan and Jake on the other as they served themselves from the enormous pan of chicken pot pie Beatrice had made. Megan was hyper aware of the man beside her as she ate, his big, strong thigh so close to hers and shower-fresh scent radiating off him.

"So, Jake, tell us more about your business," Elle said as she scooped a bite of pot pie onto her fork.

"I train horses," he told her. "Initial under saddle work and then I also help sort out horses who've acquired bad habits later in life. I've got a client who'll be dropping off a horse for me to work with full time, and I also have several clients I work with at their own barns."

"Do you offer riding lessons?" Ruby asked.

"No," he said with a slight shake of his head. "I've only got one horse of my own."

"I got to meet him earlier," Megan said. "He's a sweetheart."

"He's a great horse." Jake looked at her, and their gazes locked for a heated moment.

"Well, I'm glad you're here," Theo said, pausing to take a drink from his beer. "It's nice to have a familiar face renting the barn."

Megan grinned at that. "I bet you're glad to have a friend here too after you've put up with the three of us for the last year."

Theo's eyebrows lifted. "Yes, I suppose now I can invite Jake up for a beer when you ladies are having a girls' night."

"Just say the word," Jake said. He seemed to have relaxed since he'd first walked into the kitchen, and Megan hoped he felt comfortable here, because while Theo was a member of the British aristocracy, things at the castle had always been relaxed. Plus, Theo and Jake were friends since childhood too, although from what Megan knew, they weren't nearly as close as she, Elle, and Ruby were, probably because Theo had attended boarding school in England. He hadn't lived full time in Virginia until last year.

"Did I see Sean and Tucker out here earlier?" Theo asked, referring to two of his and Jake's mutual friends from town.

"Yeah," Jake told him. "They helped me move today."

Megan dropped her gaze to her plate. She and Sean had gone out a few times last year...before the accident.

As they ate, conversation shifted to the pair of foster cats that had been adopted that morning and then on to Megan's upcoming trip to Florida to visit her family for Purim. It wasn't a holiday she'd ordinarily fly down for, but this year, she was using it as an excuse to see her parents, because it had been too long, and she missed them.

When Jake had cleared his plate, he stood and carried it to the sink, thanking Beatrice for the meal. "I really need to be going. Thanks again for having me up for dinner tonight."

"Glad you could join us," Theo told him.

"I'll walk you out," Megan said, standing too. She fell into step beside him as he left the kitchen.

"This place is really something," he commented, gazing into

the various rooms as they passed.

"Haven't you ever been in here before?"

He shook his head. "I usually just see Theo around town, I guess."

"I'll have to bring you back up for an official tour once you're settled in," she told him, "because it's definitely worth seeing."

"I'd like that." He turned to smile at her, re-igniting that warm, familiar tingle in her belly, before looking at something over her shoulder. "Wow."

She followed his gaze to the library. "Impressive, isn't it?"

"I'm not sure impressive even covers it." Jake walked into the room, looking around at the floor-to-ceiling bookshelves.

"You like books?"

"I love them."

"So do I." But somehow, her enthusiasm seemed to pale before the awe she saw in Jake's eyes. He was looking at the shelves of books like, if it weren't so late and she weren't standing there, he might spend hours exploring every shelf, familiarizing himself with the Langdon family's collection.

"You can borrow them if you'd like," she told him. "The library's open to all our guests and anyone staying here on the property."

"I just might do that, thanks." He led the way out of the library toward the front door.

Megan was fascinated by this new side of him. She already knew Jake the rugged horse trainer, but she'd only just met Jake the dreamy-eyed book lover. How many other sides to him lurked beneath that handsome exterior? She saw him to the door before returning to the kitchen, where her friends still lingered at the dinner table.

"So, I see you and Jake are still hot for each other," Ruby said, eyes sparkling behind her glasses.

"He's our tenant, and that would be unprofessional." Megan sat, picking up her wineglass and taking a hearty sip.

"Um…" Elle glanced at Theo with a grin. "That didn't exactly stop us."

"Just a little harmless flirtation," Megan said with a shrug. "I don't think Jake's looking for a relationship right now, and really, neither am I."

"He does have a lot on his plate," Ruby agreed.

"He does. Actually, there was something I wanted to run past you guys." Megan looked at her friends, seizing hold of a momentary burst of confidence. "What do you think about offering photography sessions to our guests? You know, now that I have my new camera?"

"I think that's a wonderful idea," Elle said enthusiastically. "I love it."

"Me too," Ruby agreed. "I see our guests outside all the time taking pictures of themselves. I bet they'd love the opportunity for a professional portrait session."

"Oh! We could offer sessions with the Fairy Tails pets too," Elle said. "They could have pictures taken with their new pet before they leave, or if they're local, they could come back for a session later on."

"Yes," Megan said, relief washing away the last of her worries. "So, you don't think it's presumptuous of me to offer sessions, when I don't really have any professional experience?"

Ruby gave her a stern look. "Meg, we've seen your work. You're more than qualified. In fact, maybe we should have you take headshots of us for the website while we're at it."

Megan ducked her face with a smile. "Yeah, okay."

"Great." Ruby stood from the table. "We'll meet tomorrow to go over all the details, and then I'll get it added to our website and the rest of our marketing materials."

Megan stood too, excitement bubbling up inside her. She was doing this, finally taking a chance at turning her hobby into something more. Now, she just had to keep working, keep practicing, keep pushing herself to improve, to make sure she didn't let her friends down. Or herself.

## 3

ake woke the next morning, momentarily disoriented as he took in his surroundings. Instead of beige-painted walls and a small bedroom full of photos—memories and memorabilia of a life not lived—he found himself this morning in an off-white room that was large and open, bare except for the boxes stacked against the wall to his left.

A blank slate.

He rolled onto his back, staring up at the ceiling. This room, this house and everything that came with it, offered him a fresh start. The possibilities filled him with a sense of energy and purpose he hadn't felt in...too long to remember.

One thing was the same here as it had been in his old bedroom, though. His cock tented the sheet at his waist, hard as it was every morning, much more optimistic about the possibility of seeing some action than Jake himself. Often, he ignored it. He was so damned tired of his own hand. It never brought anything like the pleasure he remembered experiencing when he and Alana fooled around all those years ago.

So, he began running through his daily schedule in his head, waiting for his cock to get the message and accept defeat.

Today, he needed to get down to the barn to care for the horses and turn them out to enjoy Rosemont Castle's pastures for the first time. Then, he needed to unpack. Things would pick up in a day or two once the new horse he was going to train arrived, so he needed to get the house put to order in the meantime.

His cock was not taking the hint this morning, though. As soon as he acknowledged the thought, a vision of Megan formed in his head, the way her hair had brushed against his arm when they stood beside each other in the barn yesterday, the way her brown eyes seemed to spark with energy every time she smiled. His cock surged, throbbing urgently beneath the sheet.

He reached down and gripped himself, stroking hard and fast, allowing himself the fantasy of Megan's fingers wrapped around his cock. From somewhere in the room, his phone rang, interrupting the frantic movement of his fist. He paused. Few people called him. Even fewer might call at this hour.

Reluctantly, he sat up and looked around, trying to remember where he'd left his phone last night. He followed the sound to one of the boxes stacked along the wall. Tina Robertson's name showed on the screen, and his cock promptly withered at the sight. A call from his mother-in-law was one surefire way to tame his morning wood.

Technically, she was his former mother-in-law now, but Alana's death didn't stop her parents from feeling like family to him. He hoped that never changed.

"Morning, Tina," he said as he connected the call.

"Good morning, Jake. I didn't wake you, did I?"

"Nope. You know me, always up early."

"I do know," she said with a laugh. "I wanted to catch you before you headed down to the barn, see how you were settling in and if you need anything. I thought I might bake that broccoli cheddar chicken casserole that you like so much, and Walt and I could bring you supper tonight."

"I'd like that, Tina," he said, a smile tugging at his lips. "I am a total sucker for that casserole, and I'd appreciate the company too. Thanks a lot."

While he'd rather have a few more days to settle in before he invited his in-laws over, he knew Tina needed to fuss over him. She and Walt were probably already missing him, and he missed them too. For the last ten years, he'd lived in the little cabin on their property that had been their wedding gift to him and Alana. At times, he'd felt smothered, having them so close, especially without Alana at his side. But mostly, he was fiercely grateful for their love and support and for the steady presence they'd become in his life.

"Oh, honey, you can count on us anytime," Tina said in his ear. "Is there anything else you need? I could stop at the store on our way over."

"No, no. I've got to go shopping myself today and stock up the new kitchen."

"Okay, then," Tina said. "I know you've got a million things to do, so I'll let you go, but we'll see you tonight. Around six?"

"That sounds perfect. Thanks again."

He disconnected the call and crossed the room to the adjoining bathroom. Five minutes later, he was on his way to the kitchen for coffee and to rummage through his bare pantry for something to eat before heading to the barn. And cursing himself for leaving his phone on a box last night instead of on the charger. He only had twenty percent left on his battery. And where was the charger? Damned if he knew.

At least he'd had the sense to leave the coffee maker on the counter yesterday. He plugged it in now and got it started before rummaging through the box of random stuff he'd brought over from his old pantry. Seasonings, odds and ends, half a loaf of bread.

Pathetic.

There was a light knock at the door, and he turned toward it in confusion. Walt and Tina had often knocked at his cabin, making various excuses for conversation, Tina bringing food or Walt asking for a hand with a woodworking project. But Jake hadn't expected anyone to knock on his door here at Rosemont Castle.

He glanced down at his jeans and T-shirt, making sure he was presentable, before he pulled open the door. Megan stood there wearing a purple jacket and a warm smile, a white paper bag in her hands. The sight of her sent a punch of lust through his gut stronger—and hotter—than anything he could remember experiencing in recent years. It also brought a wide smile to his face.

"Hi," she said, ducking her head slightly. "Good morning."

"Morning." It was a good one now that she'd become a part of it.

"I brought you one of Beatrice's muffins. I figured your pantry was still bare."

"It is, and you have no idea how good a muffin sounds right now," he said. "But I can't let you keep feeding me like this."

Dinner last night had been nice, relaxed and casual as she'd promised. It felt good to have friends to share a meal with, although he didn't want to take advantage of their hospitality. He was renting the barn, and food service was definitely not part of the package.

"I'll try not to make a habit of it," she said, pushing the bag into his hands. "But I didn't want you to starve either. We have a full staff in the kitchen in the mornings to prepare breakfast for our guests, so there's always a ton of food. If you're ever in a pinch, just drop in. We'll happily feed you."

"I appreciate it. Really." His stomach rumbled loudly in agreement, and Megan laughed. The sound did funny things inside him, making his pants tight and his heart light. His gaze dipped briefly to the silver pendant hanging between her breasts, the Tree of Life. She'd been wearing it yesterday too.

"How are the horses this morning?" she asked.

"I'm headed down to check on them in just a few minutes."

"Okay." She stepped back, turning to leave. "I'll let you get to it."

"Thanks again for breakfast," he said. "I'm going to turn the horses out to enjoy the sunshine, so come down later this morning if you want to see them."

Her eyes gleamed as she smiled again. "I'll do that. Thanks, Jake."

"Welcome." He watched for a moment as she walked away, still fighting a mixture of lust and warmth, that irresistible combination Megan always stirred in him. Then, he ducked back inside and stood at the kitchen counter to pour himself a cup of coffee. He opened the paper bag and pulled out the muffin she'd brought. Damn, it looked good.

He took a big bite, and hallelujah, it tasted even better than it looked. Cinnamon and sweetness exploded on his tongue, almost like coffee cake, but in muffin form. He'd have to stop by the castle later to thank Beatrice. He inhaled the muffin and sucked down his coffee, wiped down the kitchen, and headed for the barn.

As he walked toward it, the knowledge swelled inside him that this was his. Twister was inside that barn. *His horse in his barn.* The culmination of all his hard work stood before him in the red-painted structure resting in front of the lush green fields beyond. He'd get to flex his muscles training horses and then flex his mind writing books. The spare bedroom would make a perfect office, and he couldn't wait to get it set up.

He pushed the door to the barn open and was immediately greeted by a friendly knicker from Twister. The smell of hay and horse greeted him as he stepped inside, the familiar shuffle of hooves over shavings and a snort from one of the rescue horses.

"Morning, buddy," he said as Twister's chestnut face appeared over the entrance to the stall. He reached out and stroked the horse, earning himself a good-natured headbutt.

He'd owned Twister for about five years now, since he was

just a colt. Twister was one of the first horses Jake had trained, back when he was still learning the ropes himself. "Did they behave themselves last night?" he asked his horse, gesturing toward the two mares across the aisle. Twister snorted, dropping his head to check Jake's pockets.

"Sorry about that. I'll make sure to get apples when I go shopping later."

He gave Twister another pat before heading over to check on the foster horses. Both of them eyed him warily. As he approached, Dusty Star's eyes widened until he could see the whites, ears pinned against her head.

"Easy there, girl," he told her. He walked to the feed room and grabbed a handful of grain, which he offered Dusty as a token of his goodwill. She took it hesitantly from his palm, and then he stood by her stall, talking quietly until her stance had softened. She pressed her nose against the bars, sniffing at him. "You're in good hands here," he told her. "You'll see." He stroked her nose through the bars as her ears flicked rapidly.

In the next stall, Bug stood quietly facing the window at the rear, her dappled coat dotted here and there with purple antibiotic spray to treat her wounds. He slid her stall door open, talking gently to her. Almost immediately, she shuffled around to face him, ribs rippling beneath her ragged coat as she moved. Anger curled in Jake's gut to think someone had allowed her and Dusty Star to live like this, starved and filthy.

Still talking quietly to her, he allowed her to sniff him before lifting a hand to stroke her neck, staying well away from her wounds. Bug was jumpy, skin twitching beneath his fingers, eyes wide and wary. These horses didn't seem to have had much handling, and what interactions they'd had with people didn't seem to have been pleasant. He'd do his best to help change that before they went to their future homes.

Even though he hadn't known of their existence until yesterday and had initially not been thrilled about having them here, he was committed now to helping them any way he could. To that end, he treated Bug's wounds and gave her and Dusty each a flake of the hay the humane society had sent over for them, a special blend that would be easy for them to digest. Colic was always a threat.

Twister hung his head over the stall door, stamping his displeasure at having been left out. "Jealous?" Jake asked. "Don't be. You're about to go graze on all the grass you can eat."

Jake gave his horse a rub and then walked out to survey the available pastures. He would turn Twister out separately from the rescue mares. The back pasture seemed to be the largest, so he'd let Twister stretch his legs there. Bug and Dusty wouldn't be able to handle much grass in their condition, so he'd put them out in the dirt riding ring today with more hay to munch on. Later, he'd give them a few minutes in one of the front pastures to graze. Gradually, over the next few weeks, he would increase their pasture time.

He spent some time familiarizing himself with the pastures and making sure there weren't any holes or other hidden dangers for the horses, then filled the water trough in the back pasture and dragged an empty trough to the riding ring, where he filled it for the rescue horses.

He brought Twister out first. The horse lifted his head as he walked out of the barn, ears pricked, nostrils flared, taking in his new surroundings. "You're going to enjoy this," Jake told him. He led Twister through the open gate and unclipped his lead line. Twister paused for a moment before setting off at a jog, chestnut coat gleaming beneath the sun.

Jake leaned against the fence, watching his horse explore the new pasture. Twister went for a run, stretching his legs and kicking up his heels, before settling down to the ever impor-tant task of grazing on the thick, green grass at hand. After a few minutes, Jake went back inside the barn. He set up the tack room and mucked Twister's stall before bringing the mares outside.

They stood in the sunlight, looking around uneasily before

beginning to munch on their hay. Twister whinnied a hello from the back pasture, but Dusty and Bug ignored him for now. Jake turned to see Megan walking toward him on the path from the castle.

"How are they doing?" she asked.

"As well as we could hope for, I think," he said. "They're pretty wary of me at the moment, but I think they'll settle down now that they're here."

"Why'd you put them in the riding ring?" She looked over at the empty pastures next to the one where Twister was grazing.

"Too much grass could cause them to colic or founder. I don't want to make them sick."

"Thank goodness you're here," she said quietly, coming to stand beside him at the fence. "We wouldn't have had the first clue what to do with them without you."

"I'm sure you'd have figured it out, but it's for the best that they have someone with experience to look after them."

She glanced at him. "Definitely for the best."

They stared at each other for a moment, during which he became hyperaware of the way the sleeve of her jacket brushed his, her cinnamon eyes reflecting the sky and pasture beyond, her skin flushed from the crisp mountain air so that it seemed to gleam. His gaze dropped to her mouth. Her pink lips were pressed together, pursed slightly as if she were contemplating something. They glistened from whatever gloss she'd applied, and he wanted to taste it, taste her. He wanted to press his lips against hers and kiss her until the aching, empty void inside him had been filled with her warm welcome presence.

"The humane society will be glad to hear they're doing so well," she said, snapping him back to reality before he did something completely ridiculous, like kiss her right here beside the pasture. "Do you have their number?"

"No, I don't."

"I'll text it to you," she said.

"I'd appreciate that."

"Okay, well, I'll let you get back to work, but you might see me down here again later."

"Stop by whenever you'd like," he said, returning his gaze to the horses grazing peacefully before them. "Bring a couple of apples, and I bet you'll be best friends in no time."

"Good to know. Bye, Jake."

"Goodbye." He resisted the urge to watch her walk away, instead striding back toward the barn to get on with his day.

MEGAN LEFT THE CASTLE MID-AFTERNOON, camera in hand and a smile on her face that the day had warmed up enough to allow her to venture outside without a jacket. It was a gorgeous March afternoon, rich with the promise of spring. Birds sang, and buds covered the trees along the walkway, promising an explosion of greenery to come.

She couldn't wait to photograph the gardens with her new camera once everything had bloomed. Already, she could see fresh green sprouts dotting the flower beds. Sucking in a deep breath of fresh mountain air, she made her way down the path toward the barn. Dusty Star and Bug weren't much to look at yet, but they were perfect candidates for a series of "before and after" photos to document their progress. Hopefully, they were still outside.

Megan hummed to herself as she walked. Her gaze roamed the pastures beyond, spotting the rescue horses near the barn, heads down as they munched on their hay. She turned her head to see Jake's horse galloping toward her across the field to her left. His coat gleamed a brilliant red beneath the sun, sleek and shiny. He slowed to a walk as he approached the fence, hanging his head over with a snort that clearly said, "get over here and pet me."

She was only too happy to comply. Twister nudged her arm, eyeing the bag of apples and carrots she carried. "Not exactly shy, are you?" she asked as she rubbed her free hand over the white blaze on his face. In response, Twister stomped a hoof and nibbled at the bag.

"For the record, I was planning to give you one anyway," she said as she pulled an apple out of the bag. Twister grabbed at it with his mouth, and she snatched her hand away, imagining her fingers getting caught between his alarmingly large teeth and the fruit. The apple dropped to the ground, and Twister gave her a reproachful look. "Sorry, big guy. I'm new at this. Don't bite me, okay?"

She picked up the apple, this time holding carefully to one side of it while the horse took a bite. He crunched happily, head bobbing up and down as Megan held onto a slobbery half of an apple. She offered it to him gingerly, jerking her fingers out of reach as soon as Twister had taken hold of it.

"Flat palm," Jake said from behind her.

She spun, heart racing at the sight of him. "What?"

"Twister's gentle, but if you're worried about getting bitten, it's easiest to feed them by holding the treat on a flat palm. Makes it easier for them to grab the food and not you."

"Good to know."

"You going to take some pictures?" he asked, gesturing to the camera slung over her shoulder.

She nodded. "I thought it would be a good idea to take some 'before and after' pictures of the rescue horses for the website. We've done that with a few of the dogs, and it's been really popular with our guests."

He fell into step beside her as she walked toward the rescue horses. "That sounds like a good idea."

They arrived at the riding arena, and Jake helped her improve her technique as she fed apples to Bug and Dusty. Both horses hung out near the fence after she'd fed them, waiting to see if she had more. Using their interest as ammunition, she snapped several closeups of each horse as well as full body shots to show their poor condition. "Dusty is going to be a stunner when she fattens up," she murmured as she worked.

The horse was a rich tan color with a black mane and tail. She had a small star-shaped white mark on her forehead that had no doubt inspired her name.

"That's for sure," Jake agreed. "I don't know if either of them have had any training, but if they can be ridden, they ought to find homes pretty quickly."

"That's a pretty big deal, isn't it?" she asked. "Whether or not they can be ridden?"

"Definitely. There are people out there looking for a companion animal to keep another horse company in the pasture, but there are a *lot* more people looking for a horse they can ride."

"Fingers crossed, then."

"You know what I do for a living, right?" Amusement laced his tone.

"Well, yes, but you have paying clients you need to focus on. The humane society can't afford to pay you for any training for these guys."

"I do have obligations, but I'll see if I can't put in a little work with them too."

"Just don't take any time away from your paying clients." She turned to face him. "Really. I know this move is a big deal for you, and the last thing I want to do is put more work on your plate."

"I appreciate that. I wasn't thrilled about the idea yesterday, but now that they're here, I'm invested in seeing them succeed. I'll do what I can."

"You're one of the good ones, aren't you?" Her voice dropped without her permission, sounding breathless and flirty, and somehow, they were standing a lot closer to each other than she remembered being a few minutes ago. Jake's arm brushed hers, the warmth of his skin radiating through her.

"I don't know about that." His eyes seared into hers before he turned his gaze back to the horses. "I reckon I owe the Robertsons for any good you see in me."

"Your in-laws?" she asked, vaguely remembering having heard that name around town, and he nodded. "It's great that you're still so close. They say tragedies either bring people together or tear them apart."

"There's a lot of truth in that." He kept his eyes on the horses, but something in his demeanor had shifted, and she regretted her inadvertent dive into personal territory.

"I'm sorry. I didn't mean to bring up anything painful," she murmured.

"Don't be," he said. "Honestly, I'm sick to death of people tiptoeing around me. I don't mind talking about it."

"Okay," she said, touched by his honesty.

"But yeah, Alana's parents have become more of a family to me than my own. I don't know how I would have gotten through any of this without them."

"I'm glad you have them." Her eyes darted to his left hand. When they'd met that night at Bar None last summer, he'd still been wearing a wedding ring, although she hadn't noticed it right away or she never would have flirted with him. Today, his hand was bare, his fingers calloused and roughened from years on the farm. A shiver passed through her as she imagined how they'd feel on her skin.

A bug buzzed past her head, and she jumped away from it at the same time Jake turned toward her. Their chests collided, her breasts pressing into his flannel shirt, and before she really even knew what she was doing, her lips brushed his. He let out a rough sound that seemed to vibrate right through her, his hands gripping her waist, drawing her closer for a moment before returning some space between them.

*Dammit*. She'd promised herself she wouldn't do this.

"Sorry," she whispered.

"Don't be," he said as a slow smile spread across his lips, and *poof*, there went her hormones, exploding for him all over again. "I think you know I've been attracted to you since that first night we met."

"Oh." She crossed her arms over her chest, trying to calm her racing heart, because yeah, she'd been sure that night, but since he signed the lease…not so much. "Really?"

"Very much so," he said, his eyes gleaming with a kind of heat that left little doubt as to the truth of his words. "It's just… I haven't dated since my wife, and I think it might not be a good idea for us to go there, you know, now that I'm living here."

"Right," she said, nodding. "You're definitely right. It could be tricky. And…maybe you're not even ready."

"I might not be." Sadness flickered across his features, and Megan's brain clicked up to speed, because Jake had just told her he hadn't been with anyone since his wife. Alana had been in a coma for something like nine years, which meant…was it possible Jake hadn't had sex since he was a teenager?

*Holy shit.*

That was…she couldn't even wrap her brain around it. Maybe, hopefully, *surely* he'd had a few random hookups in there somewhere.

"I should go." She pressed the bag of apples into his hands. "You should keep these in the barn. I'll see you tomorrow."

"Tomorrow," he echoed, and she wondered why walking away felt so hard. Maybe she was finally learning what it felt like to make mature decisions.

# 4

---

$\mathcal{D}$uchess arrived the following morning. The two-year-old gray quarter horse filly would be under Jake's care for the next month or two as he started her under saddle and trained her for western pleasure. He settled her in the stall next to Twister, knowing that both horses had calm, easygoing personalities and would likely enjoy each other's company. Indeed, after some spirited stomping and snorting, they settled in to munch hay next to each other.

"Nice place," Mr. Nichols, Duchess's owner, commented. He was a corporate CEO who'd moved to the area from Richmond a few years ago after he'd retired at the ripe old age of forty-five. Now he dabbled in the stock market and seemed to be doing well for himself, judging by the size of the property he lived on and the quality of the horses he bought for his family. Duchess was a recent acquisition, meant for his thirteen-year-old daughter Kassie to ride, and Mr. Nichols had spared no expense, ensuring the filly had the finest pedigree money could buy.

"I'm really happy to be here," Jake told him. "And grateful for the opportunity to work with Duchess."

"I wouldn't have her trained by anyone else," he said.

"You've done exceptional work with all of our horses, and we're happy to help support you in your new endeavor here at Rosemont Castle."

"Thank you, sir. It means a lot." Jake had first met the Nichols family when he worked at the Twin Pine Stables in nearby Masonville, and he couldn't be more grateful for their business. Satisfied clients like the Nichols' would tell their friends and hopefully help establish his career as a trainer. Jake had a number of clients that he visited for training sessions at their own barns, but the horses he boarded and trained at Rosemont Castle would be his real bread and butter.

The rest of the week passed relatively uneventfully. Jake spent his mornings at the barn and his afternoons in his office, working on his next book. He'd started writing on a whim during those long days at Alana's bedside. Since he'd always loved crime novels, he'd started a series starring an equine-loving private investigator who accepted cases all over the world solving crimes tangled up in the world of horses.

He couldn't say his books had been a runaway success, but they brought in enough extra income to allow him to move into his own barn a few years earlier than he would have been able to if he'd been dependent on income from horse training alone.

When he wasn't working at the castle, he traveled to his offsite clients for training sessions. He kept himself as busy as possible, throwing himself into his work on both fronts. Being here at Rosemont Castle had reinvigorated him. In fact, he couldn't remember the last time he'd felt this alive, certain parts of him in particular. Despite his best efforts, he couldn't stop thinking about Megan.

He tried to ignore it, but when he closed his eyes at night, he remembered the way it felt when her lips pressed against his, the way his blood pounded and his heart raced, every cell in his body blissfully, painfully alive.

It was probably for the best, then, that she had flown home

to Florida to visit her family. And after a few days without seeing her, he'd convinced himself he'd gotten his head back on straight. He couldn't control his thoughts in bed, but he could absolutely control his reaction to her in person. That is, until he returned from a trail ride on Twister Friday afternoon to find her walking out of the barn.

"Hi," he said as he walked Twister toward her.

"Hi." She grinned up at him, the sun sparkling in her eyes, and he was done for.

"How was Florida?"

"A lot warmer than it is here," she told him, rubbing her hands over her arms for effect. "It was great to spend a few days with my family, but I'm glad to be back. I guess Rosemont Castle feels like home now."

"That's a good thing, I think," he said.

"Yeah, I think so too." She walked over to stand next to Twister, rubbing his neck.

"Did you have a good...celebration?" he asked, suddenly aware that he had very little knowledge about Jewish holidays —apart from Hanukkah—and hoping he hadn't just put his foot in his mouth.

But Megan's smile only widened. "Yes, thank you. Purim's kind of like the Halloween of Jewish holidays, so we had fun. Mostly, it was good to see my family. I miss them."

"You're close, then?"

She nodded. "Very."

He swung down from Twister's back to face her, noticing the way she watched his every move. "You want to ride him?"

She looked at the saddle, hesitation warring with excitement in her eyes. "Right now?"

"Sure. I mean, if you want to. You could walk him around the riding ring. He's as steady as they come. You'd have nothing to worry about."

She nodded, stepping closer to Twister's side. "Yeah, you know what? I'd love that."

"Okay, then." He led Twister over to the mounting block, positioning him so she would have an easier time getting up. "Whenever you're ready."

She stepped up, slinging her right leg over Twister's back. As she settled into the saddle, a wide smile broke across her face. "It's been years since I've been on a horse."

Jake adjusted the stirrups for her as she got comfortable. "Just cluck to ask him to walk, say 'whoa' when you want him to stop, and steer him by laying the reins against his neck, like this." He reached up to adjust her grip on the reins, demonstrating.

"Got it." She wrapped her fingers around the pommel to find her balance, and Jake's mind tumbled straight into the gutter.

Also, his pants were suddenly too tight. So much for getting his head on straight where Megan was concerned. He stepped back, watching as she and Twister entered the riding ring, setting off for a loop around the well-trodden earth. Megan's hips swayed to the rhythm of Twister's gait, and really, what had he been thinking to put the woman he was already hot for on his horse?

Because the sight of her up there on Twister's back might be the most beautiful—and arousing—thing he'd ever seen. He could see her talking to Twister as she rode, a happy expression on her face.

"This is so much fun," she called to Jake as she and Twister passed the entrance to the arena, heading out for another loop.

He watched, transfixed, as she spent the next ten minutes walking Twister around the arena before guiding him back over to Jake.

"Thanks for the ride, dude." She reached down to pat Twister's neck. "I really enjoyed it."

"Ready to get off him?" he asked.

She nodded, looking down at the ground, her smile dimming. "Um, how…"

"Take both feet out of the stirrups, then lean forward and swing your right leg over his back. I'll help you from there."

She did as he'd said, lowering herself toward the ground as he put his hands on her hips, guiding her down. He tried very hard not to notice the dip of her waist beneath his fingers, but he didn't succeed. His cock was rock hard inside his jeans. As soon as her feet were on the ground, he stepped back.

Megan turned to face him, cheeks flushed. "Thank you. That was amazing."

"You're welcome. Just let me know if you'd like to ride him again sometime."

"I'll do that."

He shoved his hands into the front pockets of his jeans, attempting to disguise his condition. "I'd better get him back to the barn."

"Okay." She leaned in to press a quick kiss against his cheek. "Thanks again." And then she walked off in the direction of the castle.

Jake took Twister into the barn and got him settled, ignoring the lust still burning inside him. It was no use, though. As soon as he'd finished his evening chores, he strode toward the farmhouse, desperate for relief.

He stepped into the half bath just inside the front door and freed himself from his jeans. As he gripped himself, he had to hold in a grunt of pleasure, surprised by the sensation. The lack of pleasure was the reason he so often resisted the urge to jerk off. At some point over the years, it had started to feel weird to fantasize about Alana. He was a grown man now, and she hadn't touched him since she was eighteen. It had felt equally inappropriate to fantasize about other women while he was still married.

But now, images of Megan filled his brain, sending shock-waves of sensation through him. He pumped himself hard and fast, imagining her hands on his body, her fingers on his cock. He felt the beginnings of an orgasm, bigger and stronger than anything he'd experienced in years, building inside him, tingling at the base of his spine and in his balls. His breath caught, and he shut his eyes, losing himself in the fantasy. Sweat beaded on his brow, and every muscle in his body clenched.

He stilled his hand, opened his eyes, and grabbed a wad of toilet paper to catch his release. He gripped himself again, feeling an urgency he hadn't felt in years. A groan tore from his throat, and he couldn't hold back another moment. His hand moved at a frenzied pace, carrying him swiftly toward release.

"Jake?"

At first, he thought he'd imagined it. Her voice was part of the fantasy, and he stroked harder, faster.

"Jake, are you there?"

Through the haze of arousal, he became aware of knocking too. His hand stilled. His balls burned, but that was really Megan, standing at his front door, and here he was, just feet away in the half bath, pants open and seconds from coming.

His whole body clenched, surprise and need and embarrassment tangling themselves up inside him. Hands shaking, he removed the still-dry wad of toilet paper from the head of his cock. He tossed it in the trash and cautiously zipped his jeans, too uncomfortable to move another muscle.

"Jake?" she called again.

"Just a minute." He leaned against the sink, breathing heavily.

"It's Bug. I think something's wrong."

## 5

———

"Sorry to bother you," Megan said as Jake opened the door, "but I stopped by the barn to see the horses, and Bug seems...off. It's probably nothing, but I just thought I should let you know."

"How so?" he asked as he fell into step beside her. Something about him seemed off too. He looked stiff, flushed and breathless like he'd just come in from a long ride...or something.

"She just seemed restless, like she was in pain or not feeling well, and she wasn't eating her hay."

Jake frowned. "Could be colic."

"Is that serious?"

"It can be." He glanced over, and Megan's expression must have reflected the knot of worry lodged in her gut, because he added, "but it's usually not, especially if you catch it early."

He led the way into the barn, stopping at Bug's door. She stood motionless in the middle of her stall, much like the way she'd looked when Megan first saw her a few minutes ago. As they watched, she shifted her hooves and swung her head toward her belly.

"She's probably fine," Jake said, "but I'm going to check her out to be safe. What's the process for calling the vet with a foster animal?"

"Well, ideally they like you to call and clear any expenses ahead of time, so they can send you a pre-authorized form to give the vet for payment, but in an emergency, we can treat first and ask later."

"Okay." He walked to the room at the end of the hall where he kept his supplies, returning with what looked like a small, plastic toolbox. "I'm going to take her vitals and listen to her gut, and we'll take it from there. Will you hold her for me while I examine her?"

"Yeah, of course." She followed him into Bug's stall, accepting the lead line after he'd fastened Bug's halter.

"Hey there, girl. How're you feeling?" He spoke to Bug in a low, soothing voice as he took out a stethoscope. He stood beside her, talking and stroking her until Bug's stance softened. Still talking gently to her, he bent and pressed the stethoscope against her belly just behind her front legs, checking his watch as he took her pulse. He then placed the stethoscope against her flank near her hind legs, moving it around periodically as he listened through the earpiece. Bug tossed her head.

Jake spent the next ten minutes or so examining her, and Megan felt less silly about calling him down to the barn the longer he spent with Bug, because if she wasn't mistaken, he looked worried now too.

"Her pulse is slightly elevated, and I'm not hearing much going on in her gut. Looks like colic to me," he said at length as he put away the stethoscope and removed Bug's halter. "I'm going to put a call in to my vet and see what he recommends. I imagine he'll want to come out and see her, given her recent medical history. Do you mind calling the humane society and letting them know what's going on?"

"I'll call right now." She spent the next few minutes on the phone while Jake talked to his vet. The humane society volunteer she spoke to told her to go ahead and do anything that needed to be done, but to call back before taking any drastic—or drastically expensive—measures.

"He's on his way now," Jake said when he hung up. "You did really well to spot this so early. Colic isn't always easy to see, especially to someone without training. I wasn't planning to come back down to the barn for a few hours, and by then she could have gotten much worse."

Megan felt oddly proud at the compliment. "What is colic, exactly?"

"A stomachache, more or less. Could be a pocket of gas in her gut or a blockage. She's had some major changes to her diet since she was rescued, and I've been keeping a close eye on her and Dusty for just that reason. There isn't any manure in her stall, although that isn't necessarily a bad sign because she's only been in it for a couple of hours. She could have gone outside earlier."

The next hour was a blur of activity as the vet arrived and examined Bug. He gave her some pain medication and mineral oil to help soften up whatever might be inside her but didn't seem to think she was in any immediate danger. He left them with very specific instructions for care and monitoring her over the next twelve hours and a promise to be back first thing in the morning to reexamine her.

"Not the first night I've spent in the barn with a colicky horse and won't be the last either," Jake said as they led Bug out of the barn for a slow walk around the grounds to see if that would help stimulate some movement in her gut.

"I'd be happy to stay with her," Megan offered, feeling somewhat helpless over the situation and guilty for bringing in sickly horses that were causing so much extra work for Jake, not to mention worry for Bug herself. Megan had spent a lot of time in the barn and out in the pasture with her in the week and a half since she'd arrived.

"I don't mind," Jake said. "We could really get away with coming down to check on her every hour, but with her history,

I'd like to keep a closer eye on her, just to be safe. I'll bring my laptop down and work most of the night, probably. I've done it many times."

"What part of your work can be done on a laptop?" she asked as they walked down the path that led behind the pastures alongside the edge of the forest.

Jake glanced over at her, something guarded in his expression.

"I didn't mean to pry," she added, turning her gaze to Bug, who loped along between them, head down and looking fairly apathetic about this turn of events.

"You didn't. I brought it up. It's just not something I share with many people, but I supplement my income from horse training as an author."

Megan felt herself grinning like a fool. "An author? That's so cool. What kind of books do you write? Are you secretly famous?"

He was already shaking his head, a smile tugging at his lips. "Not famous. You've probably never heard of me. I write mysteries as Jake Tappen. It was my father's last name."

"Hmm." The name didn't sound familiar, but she couldn't wait to look him up as soon as she was back at the castle. "You're full of surprises."

"Started writing while I was sitting at Alana's bedside, and it turns out I'm pretty good at it," he said with a shrug.

"Seems like you're pretty good at a lot of things." And why did that come out sounding suggestive when she absolutely hadn't meant it that way? It wasn't like she even knew if he was good at *those* things. Her lips had barely brushed his. Heat crawled over her skin at the memory of their barely-there kiss.

"Training horses is my primary focus, but I really enjoy writing too, so I'll keep both careers going as long as I can."

"Kind of like me managing Rosemont Castle while I grow my photography business."

"A lot like that, actually." Jake gave her a warm smile that made her go all gooey inside.

"Truthfully, Elle's handling most of the property management details these days while Ruby works on her web development business and I focus on photography. We all help out with the day-to-day stuff, but this way we each get to focus on what we enjoy."

"That's the way to do it," he agreed.

Bug snorted, as if to remind them they were supposed to be paying attention to her. Megan reached over and rubbed her neck as she walked. "She's going to be okay, isn't she?"

"She's not out of the woods yet, but yeah, I think she'll be okay. Doc Kaminski didn't see anything too concerning when he examined her."

"I don't want to lose her," Megan admitted quietly.

"Well, neither do I. She's just starting her second chance here."

"Hear that, Bug?"

The horse made no response, walking quietly between them. The truth was, Bug wasn't the only one starting her second chance here at Rosemont Castle. The same might be said about Megan herself, and Jake too. She hoped they all found what they were looking for. They rounded the farmhouse and walked quietly back to the barn.

"Time to put her in her stall and let her rest for a while. If you don't mind holding her for a minute, I'm going to get rid of her hay."

"She can't eat it?" Megan asked.

He shook his head. "She shouldn't eat hay until the colic has passed. We can try to tempt her with some grass later, though. It's got enough moisture in it to help get things moving again for her, but if she does have a blockage, hay could make it worse."

"Gotcha."

He went into her stall with a pitchfork, returning a minute

later with Bug's hay. The horse watched with idle interest, but if Megan wasn't mistaken, her eyes were a little more alert and inquisitive than they had been earlier. Megan, pleased with the horsemanship she'd learned so far, walked Bug into her stall and removed her halter.

"Nicely done," Jake said. "Now we wait."

Megan rubbed Bug again before walking out to the aisle and closing her stall door.

"Just need to keep an eye on her for any further signs of distress, walk her every few hours, and offer her some grass while we're out. I'll probably set up a chair here by her stall for the night."

"Could I stay too?" she asked, reluctant to leave Bug just yet, or maybe her reluctance to leave had more to do with Jake than Bug. "Or do you need to work?"

He looked over, his expression intense and heated. "I'd enjoy the company."

～

JAKE SAT in the aisle of the barn, leaning back against the rough wooden side of Bug's stall. Megan settled herself beside him with a sigh. He'd spread several thick horse blankets on the floor for them to sit on. If he got tired later, he might lay back and nap here.

Behind them, Bug shifted restlessly in her shavings. Jake couldn't quite shake the guilt that had nagged at him since Megan showed up at his door. If he hadn't been so distracted by his attraction to her earlier, he would have noticed Bug's colic himself.

What if Megan hadn't come to check on her? Or if she hadn't recognized Bug's discomfort? He was responsible for these horses' welfare while they were in his barn, and he couldn't allow himself to get distracted like this again.

"Hungry?" Megan gestured to the basket she'd brought

down from the castle while he was getting them set up here in the barn.

"Starving. What've you got?"

"Chicken tortilla soup," she said.

"Sounds good right about now," he said. The temperature had dropped now that the sun had set, and the promise of filling his belly with something hot sounded perfect.

"I thought so too." She lifted two thermoses out of the basket and handed him one. "There's fresh bread in here too, and a whole stash of peanut butter cookies. Beatrice said we'd need fuel to make it through the night."

"You don't have to stay the night," he told her.

"I know." Her eyes flicked to his. "But I don't think I'd sleep a wink if I went back up to the castle, worrying about her."

"I know that feeling." He screwed the top off his thermos and snagged a spoon from the open basket. A rich, slightly spicy scent filled the air. "It smells good."

They slurped soup in silence, both of them hunched over their thermoses to keep from making a mess. Behind them, Bug watched, head down, eyes droopy. Across the aisle, Twister hung his head over his stall door, giving them a curious look. When they'd finished the soup and the bread, they dug into the cookies.

"I saw you out with Duchess this morning," Megan said as she brushed cookie crumbs off her lap. "She looks like she's coming along nicely."

As if she'd heard her name, Duchess hung her head out of the stall next to Twister's, and they nipped at each other play-fully. Although the horses usually stayed outside overnight, Jake had brought them in tonight to help keep Bug company in the barn.

That morning, he'd worked Duchess on the lunge line in a bridle and saddle with the stirrups removed. "She's almost ready for me to get on her back. She's so steady, I don't think it'll take her long to get used to it. Plus, I've been letting her watch me tack up Twister and ride him, so she knows what's coming."

Megan leaned back against Bug's stall. "I have a feeling we'll both be exhausted tomorrow, but another day, let me know when you're going to work with her, and I'll come down and take some pictures for your website."

"That would be great. Thank you."

"Of course. She's absolutely gorgeous. She should photograph really well. Yeah, I'm complimenting you," she said to Duchess, who was watching them with wide, curious eyes. "You look like a million bucks."

"You're not far off," Jake told her. "She's by far the most valuable horse in the barn."

"Damn, girl," Megan said to the filly. "Well, only fitting you should live at a castle, then."

"Until she goes back to the mansion she came from."

Megan shook her head with a smile. "I guess I never thought about horses having value before. That's kind of weird, isn't it? To say she's worth more than Dusty and Bug, who'll get adopted for a hundred bucks or so?"

"Horses are property, an asset to people like the Nichols who own Duchess. She's insured, as are all their horses, in case anything happens to her."

Megan's eyebrows lifted. "Wow. I had no idea."

"People spend a lot of money in the horse industry."

"How did you get started in it?" she asked. "You told me before you kind of fell into it by accident."

"Needed a way to earn cash when I was too young to work anywhere legally." It felt like a lifetime ago, when he'd mucked stalls to help his mother pay the bills, not realizing he was actually supporting her drug habit. "Alana rode at the stable where I worked. That's how we met."

"Aw," Megan said softly, reaching over to squeeze his hand. "Is her family wealthy, then?"

"A lot wealthier than mine, but they're not rich. Upper middle class, I'd say."

"What happened?" she asked, scooting closer to him on the blanket. "If you don't mind me asking. I know she fell soon after your wedding."

"During the wedding reception," he corrected her. "It was just one of those freak things. She tripped on her dress and fell down some steps behind the VFW hall, hit her head on the concrete. She never regained consciousness."

"During the wedding reception," Megan repeated, pressing a hand over her mouth. "Oh, Jake, I'm so sorry. That's awful."

"That first night, it was all so terrifying. I begged, and I prayed for her to survive. We all prayed so hard, and we thought our prayers had been answered when she made it through the night."

Megan was silent, her hand on his arm in support.

"But I didn't realize the real nightmare had just begun, watching her waste away in that hospital bed. I don't think she would have wanted what her life became."

"Those decisions must be the very hardest to make," she said quietly.

"It's not like we'd ever talked about end of life wishes or anything. I mean, we were only eighteen. We were all so desperate to save her. We would have done anything to keep her alive those first weeks, months even. Her parents never gave up on a miracle, but at some point over the years, I realized we were just watching her die. Years and years of watching her die."

Megan wrapped her arms around him. "I honestly can't even imagine. No one should have to."

"I wish like hell I didn't," he admitted. "I feel like I spent nine years dying alongside her."

"You put your whole life on hold," she whispered. "Alana was a lucky woman to have a husband like you. I'm sorry she never got the chance to live the life you guys had planned together."

"It's a strange position to be in." He tucked Megan's head under his chin, enjoying the freedom to hold her, realizing how long it had been since he'd experienced the simple pleasure of holding someone like this. "I mourned her when she died, but in some ways, it felt like I had already mourned her. I've essentially been alone for ten years. I haven't...I feel embarrassingly out of practice at anything a man my age should be experienced in."

And that admission, uttered in an otherwise silent barn with Megan nestled against his chest and several horses watching in idle curiosity, left him feeling raw.

She lifted her head, her gaze dropping to his lips. "That's a hell of a thing."

"It is." He laughed, surprising himself at the unexpected reaction.

"You may be out of practice at a few things because you were faithful to your wife, but I'm sure it will all come back to you when the time comes." She sat up, resting a hand on his shoulder. "And you're experienced enough in other areas to make up for it. You've lived through more than most people do in a lifetime already, Jake. You've got to be as tough as a...what are those big horses in the Budweiser commercial called?"

"Clydesdale?"

"You're as tough as a Clydesdale, inside and out. You're going to do amazing things with your life, now that you actually have the chance to live it."

egan shivered as she and Jake walked out of the barn with Bug between them. "Imagine if we'd taken Bug and Dusty in without having rented the stables and were trying to do this by ourselves?"

"Your instincts were spot on tonight. You'd have known to call the vet."

They walked another loop around the property. It was past midnight now, and her fingers were numb inside her gloves by the time they made it back to the barn.

"I'm going to go put on a pot of coffee," Jake said after he'd gotten Bug settled in her stall. "If you don't mind watching her for a few minutes."

"Not at all. I think coffee is definitely going to be necessary tonight."

"Lots of it." With a quick smile, he strode off in the direction of the farmhouse.

Megan sat on their bed of horse blankets, drawing her knees against her chest. She watched as Bug shifted her weight from one hoof to another, hoping the little horse would be okay. In the time she'd spent at Rosemont Castle, Bug had clearly put on weight. Her ribs were far less prominent now than they had been when she arrived. Her wounds looked better too, although they were still stained a bright purple from the disinfectant spray. Surely, she would pull through this setback...

Naively, Megan had imagined taking in a couple of low-maintenance horses and fostering them for a few weeks before they went on to new homes. In reality, it would be weeks before Bug and Dusty were even available for adoption. First, they both had a whole lot of getting healthy to do, although Bug was clearly the more delicate of the two.

"You feeling any better yet?" she asked the horse.

Bug spun, hanging her head over the open top of the stall door, her soft muzzle nudging the top of Megan's head where she sat on the floor. She lifted a hand and rubbed Bug's nose. The skin there was so much softer than it looked, and fuzzy, almost like velvet.

"I like you too," she said, hoping Bug's gesture meant what she thought it did. "I think we'll be good friends once you're feeling better."

"I'd say you already are," Jake said from the doorway, a travel mug of coffee in each hand. Bug raised her head to look at him but didn't step away from the doorway to her stall. Jake walked over, handing one of the mugs to Megan before stroking Bug's face. She bobbed her head up and down a few times before moving off to the far side of her stall.

"Feel free to use the farmhouse for anything you need, kitchen, bathroom, or just a place to warm up for a few minutes," Jake said.

"Actually, I'll take you up on that." She sipped her coffee and set it on the floor. "I could use a bathroom, and it's a lot closer than the castle."

He nodded. "Take your time."

She stood and walked out of the barn toward the little white house at the other end of the driveway. The front door was unlocked so she let herself in, heading for the half bath just inside the front door. She used the facilities and then wandered into the living room, where she flicked on the gas fireplace and stood for a few minutes warming her fingers and toes.

She'd been in the farmhouse a lot while they got it fixed up to rent, and the difference now was striking. With Jake's stuff here, it looked like a home. His furniture was minimalistic, no pictures on the walls—or none yet anyway—but he'd left out enough things to make the place look lived in, a book here, coffee mug there.

She imagined him kicked back on the couch, jean-clad legs stretched along the cushions, a beer in one hand. Or maybe the beer would be on the coffee table while he held his laptop, busily writing the next chapter of his latest novel. There was a whole lot more to Jake Reardon than she'd first realized, and she liked all of it.

A lot.

Deciding she'd dawdled in his house long enough, she shut off the fireplace and walked to the stable. Jake sat on the pile of horse blankets in the aisle, much as she'd just been picturing him in his home—legs stretched out in front of him and a coffee mug in one hand. He was turned away from her, talking over his shoulder to Bug, whose head was hanging over her stall door, watching him intently.

If only Megan had her camera with her. She would have given anything to capture that moment, the image of this big, strong man sitting on the floor with the sickly, scarred rescue horse gazing down at him, a trusting, affectionate look on her face.

Megan's heart melted into a puddle of lovesick goo in her chest.

"Looks like you're all settled into the farmhouse," she said quietly to alert him to her presence.

He turned his head, a relaxed smile on his face. "Easy to do when you don't bring much with you."

"I suppose that's true." She sat beside him, reaching for her coffee, then gestured at Bug. "She looks like she's feeling better."

"She does. I checked her over while you were inside, and her vitals are good, although I'm still not hearing much activity in her gut. We may just be seeing the effects of the pain medication making her more comfortable."

Megan sobered. "Damn."

Jake rested a hand on hers. "I still think she's going to be fine, but we're not out of the woods yet."

"How will we know?"

"Well, if she poops, that'll be a great sign," he said with a sardonic grin.

She returned it with one of her own. "Great. Here we are, sitting in the barn at one in the morning, waiting for a horse to poop."

"It's a glamorous life."

She leaned against the wall of Bug's stall, allowing her shoulder to bump into Jake's. "Earlier, you said you didn't share the fact that you're an author with many people. Why is that?"

He shrugged. "No real reason. I just don't like to make a fuss."

Yeah, she could see that about him. "I bet Theo has your books in his library."

"He does. I saw them there when I was poking around last week."

"You really like that library, huh?"

He gave her an amused look. "Yeah, I do."

"I haven't spent too much time in it, but I'm going to go find your books," she told him. "And I'm going to read them too."

Jake looked away, adorably uncomfortable with her attention. "If you do, don't tell me."

"I'm not making any promises."

They continued to make idle chitchat as the night wore on. Eventually, they fell quiet as fatigue set in. Behind them, Bug dozed in her stall. Megan felt herself losing the battle and decided there was no reason for her not to doze too. Her eyes closed, and she drifted off into a light but exhausted sleep.

The next thing she knew, a buzzing sound jolted her awake, and...what in the world? She opened her eyes to find herself sprawled across Jake's sleeping form. Her arms were wrapped around his chest, one of her legs nestled into the space between his thighs.

Was she still dreaming? Because how...what...

But no, his eyes opened too, looking similarly confused. He shoved a hand into the pocket of his jeans and pulled out his cell phone, silencing the alarm that had awoken them. Then, he raised up on his elbows, looking behind him at Bug's stall. She was visible in the doorway, dozing peacefully.

"Set it in case we fell asleep, so I wouldn't miss checking on Bug." His voice was deep and gravelly, and he made no move to get out from under her.

"Um." She was disoriented from sleep, but certain parts of her were one-hundred-percent awake and hyper-aware of the contact with bits of Jake she'd never touched before, especially the parts that brought her into contact with the crotch of his jeans.

"I...guess we got cold in our sleep?" He offered, still making no effort to move.

"I do feel awfully warm right now," she said, but it came out as more of a whisper because his cock was rapidly hardening against her thigh, and suddenly she couldn't move, couldn't breathe, couldn't think past the lust muddling her brain, sending pulses of need straight to her core.

Her head dipped as his rose, lips meeting in a crushing kiss.

JAKE SANK his hands deep into the mahogany depths of Megan's hair as their mouths met. Her tongue slid along the seam of his lips, and he opened to her, surrendering to the overpowering

58

need inside him, the need to be touched and kissed, to allow himself the things he had so long been denied. A low groan tore from his throat as her tongue stroked his.

As recently as five minutes ago, he had forgotten anything could feel so good. He felt supercharged as his body awoke to the intense pleasure of a woman's touch, the warmth of her body covering his, the whisper of her breath against his cheeks as they kissed. Somehow, he thought nothing had ever felt as wonderful as this moment with Megan.

"You feel so good," he mumbled, allowing his hands to roam down her back, settling on her waist, memorizing every dip and curve of her body.

She shifted above him, and suddenly his cock was pressed into the heat between her legs. His grip tightened on her waist, holding her in place, too exquisitely aroused to move.

So good. *Too* good...

After ten years without so much as a kiss, a lifetime without experiencing the full pleasure of a woman's body, Jake's control was frayed beyond repair. Megan was still kissing him, unaware of the battle raging inside him, the intense need for more, more, *more*, warring with the knowledge that his body wouldn't tolerate too much more of this without demanding release.

"Haven't stopped thinking about you all week." He slipped his palms beneath her jacket, inside her top, finding the hot, smooth skin of her lower back. So incredibly soft, so much softer than his own.

"Me neither," she whispered as she trailed a path of hot kisses across his jaw to his neck, where she nipped lightly.

"Fuck." His hips jerked as a bolt of pure fire shot through his cock. "Need you so bad."

"I can tell." She lifted her head to meet his gaze, a wicked smile on her face, as she rolled her hips up and down his length.

He hissed out a breath, hands pressing against her lower

back, holding her close, silently begging her to keep going, and she did, hips moving rhythmically against his as they kissed, deep and sloppy and desperate. How had he gone ten years without this? Screw that. How had he gone ten months, ten weeks, ten days...

Maybe he'd forced himself to forget, or maybe he'd never experienced anything quite as intensely erotic as the feel of Megan's body moving so beautifully against his. But he was awake now, every cell in his body achingly alive in a way he might not have ever felt but would certainly remember for the rest of his life.

"Jake?" She stilled, staring down at him, something hesitant lurking in her eyes.

"Yeah?" He stroked the skin just above the waistband of her jeans.

"Has it really been ten years?" she whispered, her expression achingly kind.

He nodded. "Feels more like a million right now."

There was a clunk and a snort from the stall behind them, reminding him what they were supposed to be doing right now, which was definitely *not* making out on a pile of horse blankets in the aisle of the barn. He sat up slowly, drawing Megan into his lap as he craned his head to look at Bug. She stood motionless in the middle of the stall, looking no better or worse than she had the last time he checked on her.

Megan followed his gaze, staring silently at the horse for a few long seconds. "I have no idea how you've managed."

He huffed a bitter laugh. "It hasn't been easy, and I'm not just talking about sex. I didn't realize how much I'd missed just...touching someone."

She snuggled against his chest, looping an arm over his shoulder. "Like this?"

"Yeah. Been a long time since I held someone. Feels good."

"Even with..." She gestured to the painfully obvious bulge in his jeans.

"Even with that." And it wasn't a lie either. No matter the obstacles between them, his virginity or living on the property she managed, they couldn't have had sex tonight anyway. They had to watch over Bug until she'd recovered from her colic.

"It's been a little while for me too," she said softly, her face pressed into his jacket. "I mean, not nearly as long...but a year or so, which for me, is a really long time."

"Why's that?" he asked. "The break from dating, I mean."

She shrugged. "I've just been focused on things here at the castle and my photography."

"You've been busy," he agreed, wondering if that was the whole story or if the car accident that left her scarred had anything to do with it.

"We're going to have to deal with this thing between us, though, aren't we?" she said, looking up at him. "I mean, one way or the other."

"I guess we will."

"Maybe not right now when it's the middle of the night, and we're half delirious and horny as hell." She winked.

"Agreed."

"So should I, um, get out of your lap?"

"No." His arms tightened around her. "You're driving me ten kinds of crazy, but it feels so damn good to hold you."

"Well, I'm glad, because it feels good to be held." She rested her head against his shoulder, her voice gone quiet.

"It's been so long since I've felt this kind of physical attraction. It just feels so...I don't know what the right word is. I've felt so isolated. Sometimes I thought I'd never feel a woman's touch again, even just to sit here like this with you in my lap."

"Dammit, Jake. That's really sweet...or sad...or both. I don't know."

He grunted with laughter. "I don't want to be sweet *or* sad."

"You're not," she said. "Maybe your situation is, but you're strong and sexy and just so *good*. I'm really glad you're getting this chance to go after all the things that you've had to wait so long for and really sorry Alana couldn't be here with you for it."

"It's hard to even imagine what my life would have been like if she hadn't fallen. I mean, she was only eighteen. I don't know what she would have been like as an adult. I can't even imagine myself with her now, because I'm so much older than the only Alana I ever knew, if that makes any sense."

"I think it does, yeah." She reached down and squeezed his hand. "And I'm really glad you're willing to talk about her with me like this."

"It would be more awkward if we didn't talk about it, don't you think?"

"I do." She nodded. "Definitely."

"This might sound strange, but talking to you here tonight, and all the other stuff we did, feels like the most functional thing I've done in years."

She grinned. "I'm glad. Maybe it's been a good, functional thing for me too."

"And here I thought kissing you was a bad decision."

"Sometimes bad decisions turn out to be good ones."

## 7

---

$\mathcal{M}$egan rolled over in bed, groaning as her face encountered something rough and scratchy, and why was she so cold? Her eyes popped open, and a red wool horse blanket came into focus before her bleary eyes. Right. Night in the barn.

*Making out in the barn...*

A grin tugged at her lips as she pushed herself up to a sitting position. Dawn had brightened the sky outside, and Jake stood at Bug's stall door, watching her with a matching grin on his handsome face.

"How long was I asleep?" she asked, her voice as rough and scratchy as the blanket she'd been laying on.

"An hour or so. You needed it."

"Not gonna lie, I'm heading straight for my bed as soon as we know Bug's okay."

"I'm probably going to do the same thing." Fatigue sharpened the angles of his face and the tiny crinkles around his eyes. "The good news is that Bug just took a huge dump."

Megan giggled as she climbed to her feet. "Feeling better now?" she asked the horse as she peered into her stall. Bug lifted her head, indeed looking much perkier than she had earlier in the night. "A big load off your mind, huh?"

Jake chuckled. "Doc Kaminski will be here in a few minutes. Hopefully he'll give her the all clear."

In the meantime, they took turns visiting the farmhouse to freshen up. By the time she made it back to the barn, the vet's truck was in the driveway. She found him and Jake in the stall with Bug, examining her.

"Morning, Megan," Doc Kaminski said.

"Good morning."

"Heard you guys had a long night."

"We did, but at least she seems to be getting better. She *is* getting better, right?" she asked, worry sneaking back into her tone.

The vet nodded, an easy smile on his weathered face. "She looks good this morning. I think she's out of danger, although you'll still want to keep a close eye on her for a couple of days, and I've recommended to Jake that you limit her hay for the rest of the week." He gave Bug a pat on the rump as he left her stall. "I'll call later to check on her."

"Thanks again, Doc."

Megan was quiet as the vet left, standing beside Bug's stall. "Well, that's a relief."

He nodded. "I'd say we can safely go crash now. I'll check on her later this morning."

"I'll come down and check on her again too." She pushed Bug's stall door open and walked to the horse, resting a hand gently on her neck. "Really glad you're feeling better, kiddo."

"That makes two of us," Jake said from behind her.

She walked out of the stall, shut and latched the door, and turned to face him. "So, we should probably talk, preferably soon, before I wind up in your lap again."

He grinned. "How about dinner? My place? Say, seven tonight?"

"I'd like that." And wow, she couldn't remember the last

time a man had cooked for her, let alone *offered* to cook for her without any prompting on her part.

"See you tonight, if I don't bump into you in the barn before then." He leaned in to press a quick, gentle kiss against her lips before they walked out of the barn together, parting at the end of the driveway. He took the fork toward the farmhouse, and she climbed the lane toward the main castle.

"You look like you had a rough night," Ruby said, walking out of the parlor as Megan pushed through the castle's front doors.

"Spending the night in the barn will do that to a girl." She allowed her empty stomach to guide her straight to the kitchen.

Ruby followed, laptop tucked beneath her arm. "How's Bug?"

"Out of danger for now, although apparently we'll have to watch her more closely to keep it from happening again."

"She's okay, though?" Elle asked as she walked into the kitchen.

Megan quickly recounted her night and Bug's prognosis for her friends, as Beatrice plied them with freshly baked bagels.

"So, what did you and Jake do to pass all that time together?" Ruby asked, eyebrows climbing behind her glasses.

"Um." Megan could feel the flush spreading over her skin. "A little of that, yeah."

"What?" Ruby said, her voice rising to a squeal. "I was just joking, Meg. Holy shit, what did you guys do?"

"Kissed, messed around some. He hasn't…" She rubbed at the fatigue-induced headache building behind her eyes. "You know about his wife, and well, she was in a coma for nine years…"

"He hasn't been with anyone since his wife died?" Elle asked.

Megan shook her head. "So that's…a lot to think about."

65

"It is," Ruby agreed. "In fact, I say we need a girls' night to discuss before you take this any farther."

"Any excuse for girls' night sounds good to me," Elle said.

"Yeah," Megan agreed. Now that she was back at the castle, dinner with Jake tonight felt like too much, too soon. Ruby was right. She *did* need to talk this through with her friends before she made any decisions. "Let's do it."

JAKE WALKED into the farmhouse and headed straight for the bedroom. He sat on the bed, unzipped his jacket, and tossed it aside. It felt good to sit on something soft. He needed sleep, but before he could sleep, he needed a shower. Was Megan doing the same thing right now, undressing for a shower before she climbed into bed? The image formed in his head before he could stop it, followed by a vivid memory of the way it had felt to hold her in his arms and kiss her, the intense pleasure of her hips grinding against his.

His cock hardened inside the confines of his jeans. He needed release. Desperately. All thoughts of a shower or sleep now forgotten, he lay back on the bed and unzipped his jeans, fisting himself, imagining that he was back in the barn with Megan. Instead of the mattress beneath him, it was Twister's red winter blanket, and she was riding him hard and fast. This was his fantasy after all, so the reasons they hadn't actually had sex in the barn didn't matter.

He imagined sinking deep inside her, hips thrusting against hers as he barreled toward the finish line. And since it was only a fantasy, he didn't care that he wasn't going to last long, because his orgasm was already building, and all he could think about was getting there as quickly as possible.

His cell phone started to ring. He stilled his hand, glancing over at it. Megan's name gleamed on the screen, and she really had amazingly accurate timing for interrupting him. This time, he could easily let her go to voicemail, though, and carry on. But suddenly, the need to hear her voice was greater than his physical need. He released his cock, swallowing a groan.

"Hello?" His voice sounded like he'd swallowed sandpaper.

"Hi," she said. "It's Megan."

As if he could possibly mistake her voice or the fire that shot through his groin at the sound. "I know."

She laughed softly. "I figured, but…you weren't already asleep, were you?"

"Nope, not asleep." Very painfully awake.

"You sound kind of…" She drifted off, as if she'd just realized exactly what he was doing. Maybe she had. The thought only made him harder. "Did I interrupt…?"

"Not interrupting anything," he said, hearing the raw need in his voice and not much caring. His cock throbbed impatiently.

"No?" Now she sounded amused. "So, you don't mind chatting with me while I get ready for bed?"

"Can't," he growled. "Busy."

"That's what I thought." He could hear the smile in her voice. "Listen, I was just calling because it turns out I have plans tonight. Can we do dinner tomorrow night instead?"

"Sure. No problem."

"Okay. I'll let you go, then," she paused. "Oh, and Jake?"

"Yeah?"

"Think of me," she whispered.

As if he could possibly not. He slung the phone onto the table beside the bed, his fist again moving at a frenzied pace. Megan's voice in his ear, the heat of her body grinding against his…

The orgasm took him hard, pulsing through him as he came, and he came, and he came. He could hear himself swearing, fist still moving, milking every moment of his much-needed release because he hadn't come this hard—or this long—in years.

Afterward, he lay flat on his back, feet on the floor, still wearing his boots, panting and gasping for breath as blissful relief buzzed through his veins. Jesus Christ. If this was even a fraction of how good it felt to have sex, he might have just fully realized what he'd been missing.

~

MEGAN WOKE, groggy and disoriented. She squinted at the clock. Why was she in bed at noon? Slowly, the previous night came back to her. Bug's colic. Sitting in the barn with Jake. That phone call as she was climbing into bed when his voice sounded like pure sex and she was so sure she'd interrupted him jerking off that she'd had to pull out her vibrator after she got off the phone before she could fall asleep herself.

With a groan, she crawled out of bed, her body annoyingly sluggish after her disjointed sleep. She showered and dressed and spent the next hour walking not only her foster dogs, but Elle's too, to make up for Elle watching her dogs last night. As she looked at the calendar on her phone, she realized with a jolt that her first portrait session was booked for today.

She'd been anxiously anticipating it for days, and then Bug's colic had completely wiped it from her mind. A shiver ran through her, erasing the last remnants of sleep from her brain. Earlier that week, she'd scouted some potential locations, but she'd need to review them before the session. Focused now, she headed downstairs for a late lunch while tabbing through her notes. Then, she went upstairs to get her camera, giving herself a silent pep talk, before heading to the foyer.

*Here goes nothing...*

"Hi, I'm Megan Perl." She extended her hand to the young couple waiting for her there. "You must be the Chens."

And from there, it went...surprisingly well. She led them around the castle grounds, having them pose in various locations and snapping some impromptu photos of them walking and interacting with each other too. It helped that they were very much in love, giving Megan plenty of unscripted romantic moments.

When she made it back to her room afterward, she sat on the bed, tabbing through photos on the viewfinder. There were plenty of tossers—blurry photos or pictures where someone's eyes were closed—but there were also some nice shots in there, certainly enough to work with once she started editing them.

Bubbling with a restless combination of relief, excitement, and exhaustion, she left her room and walked down to the barn to check on Bug. She found the rescue horses in their usual spot in the riding arena, dozing in the sunshine. Both horses lifted their heads and stared at her as she approached.

"Hey, ladies. Long time, no see," Megan said as she walked up to the fence.

Bug walked over to greet her, allowing Megan to rub her face, careful not to come close to the bite wound on her cheek. Beneath the purple spray, the wound looked much better than it had when they'd arrived almost two weeks ago. She was healing, just as Megan had.

"Lucky for you, I don't think the boy horses will care if you have a scar on your face," Megan told her softly.

Bug flicked her ears, dropping her head to nibble at a few stray pieces of hay in the dirt.

"Hopefully potential owners won't care either." Although Megan had her doubts about that. She'd seen scarred or otherwise "imperfect" animals be looked over at the shelter in favor of the prettier ones. Human nature was what it was, after all. Megan's fingers slid over the jagged line on her face.

Sometimes…sometimes she could almost forget it was there. But it only took one awkward glance from a guest at the castle or the kid behind the register at the grocery store to remind her. And every time she looked at herself in the mirror, it was all she could see. It changed her whole face.

The scars extended down her left arm, although she knew it

was her own vanity that kept her from being as conscious of the scarring there. No one flinched when they saw her arm, not the way they did when they saw her face.

Before the accident, Megan had been the outgoing social butterfly in her group of friends. Men gravitated to her with very little effort on her part, and she basked in their attention. Now, sometimes she wasn't even sure who she was anymore.

"Just can't seem to keep you away," Jake said from behind her.

She turned, allowing her hair to fall over the left side of her face out of habit, even though Jake had seen her scars plenty of times by now. "I just wanted to check on her before I head up for dinner."

"She's doing fine." He reached out and tucked her hair behind her ear. "Dinner, huh? Who am I getting blown off for?"

"Elle and Ruby," she admitted. "Girls' night."

"Well, I can't complain about that. Want to help me bring them in?" he asked, gesturing toward the horses.

"Oh, yeah. Sure."

He lifted Bug's halter and lead line off the hook on the fence where they'd been hanging and handed them to her. "She seems to have taken to you."

"I like her too," Megan said as she fitted the halter onto Bug's head, surprised at how quickly she'd become comfortable handling the horses, Bug in particular.

Jake took Dusty Star, and together they led the two horses into the barn. The aisle was clear today, but Megan still felt a delicious heat travel over her skin as her gaze fell on the spot where she and Jake had fooled around on the horse blanket last night.

She led Bug into her stall and took off her halter, giving her one last rub before she left her. "I'll see you tomorrow, then," she said to Jake, waving over her shoulder as she left the barn. By the time she made it to the castle, Ruby was already ushering her toward the stairs for their girls' dinner up in the tower. She carried one of the platters Beatrice had prepared for them, and Megan grabbed the other one. Elle came behind them, carrying a wine tote and glasses.

"I brought three bottles tonight," Elle said.

Ruby lifted her eyebrows in question as she set the platter on her dresser and started spreading out blankets for them to sit on. Her cats, Simon and Oliver, hopped up, sniffing at the covered tray.

"I thought we might need extra wine to accompany all the gossip," Elle said. "And also, Theo left for London this morning, so I figured I might as well have a few glasses while I panic about how I have to get married in front of the whole Langdon family at their fancy estate in England."

Megan turned to her friend in surprise. "Isn't that what you wanted?"

"It is, but it isn't," Elle said with a shrug, her shoulders stiff. "I mean, you know I'm totally in love with the idea of a fairy-tale wedding, but I just...I never quite feel like I fit in when I visit their estate. Everyone's so proper and cultured. They're all born and raised in the aristocracy, and I'm...not. Some of them look down their noses at me."

"I'm sorry, Elle," Ruby said, resting a hand on her arm. "That's lousy."

"It is," Megan agreed.

"And then there's Theo's uncle George, who thinks he's making a huge mistake by living here in America and never misses a chance to rub his nose in it." By now, Elle had opened the first bottle of wine and was pouring glasses for each of them.

"Well, you can rub all *their* noses in it when you become his wife," Megan said, wrapping an arm around her friend. "And you'll have us, and your dad, and lots of other friends and family there that day to support you."

"Yeah," Elle said with a smile, her shoulders relaxing. "That's true. It'll all feel so much better with you guys there beside me."

"We've got your back, always." Ruby joined in, and they held on to each other for a group hug.

"Thanks for the pep talk, ladies." Elle swiped at her eyes. "I needed that."

"Any time," Megan told her. "That's what we're here for."

"And also for gossip," Ruby added as she raised her wineglass for a toast.

Megan and Elle leaned in to tap their glasses against hers.

"And what are we gossiping about tonight, exactly?" Megan asked.

"You and Jake," Ruby told her. "We want all the details on what happened last night in the barn. Did you guys literally go for a roll in the hay or what?"

"No hay," Megan said, swirling her wine gently, watching as it coated the glass in its ruby tint before sliding back into the bottom of the glass. "But there might have been a horse blanket involved…"

"Oh my God," Elle said with a delighted grin.

"A lot of kissing and groping, but not much more than that," Megan said. "I mean, we were there watching over Bug while she was sick, but I'm not sure we would have gone much farther anyway. He's got a lot of emotional baggage from what happened with his wife."

"And you've got some emotional baggage of your own," Elle said as she uncovered the trays, and Ruby's tower bedroom filled with the delicious scent of chicken marsala.

"What? I do not." Megan reached for a plate and began serving herself. "I've been with more guys than the two of you combined. I enjoy sex, and I make no excuses for it."

"Yeah," Elle said gently. "And how many guys have you been with since the accident?"

Megan slid her plate onto her lap, keeping her gaze firmly on the chicken. "I've been focused on my photography."

"Okay," Elle said with a shrug, "but if and when you want to talk about it, we're here."

Megan had a sudden, vivid memory of the Fairy Tails Ball they'd hosted here at the castle just a week or so after the accident. She'd flown home to recuperate with her family, making the last-minute decision to come back for the party just a few hours before it began.

She'd been in so much pain, physical and emotional, and she'd felt like Frankenstein with the bandages and makeup on her face, hiding the stitches and bruising. Ruby and Elle had held her, laughed with her and cried with her, picked her up when she felt like hiding in her bedroom for the rest of her life rather than facing the world.

"I'm fine," she insisted now. "Really."

"So, are you and Jake exploring a relationship or what?" Elle asked.

"We're having dinner tomorrow night to answer that question," Megan said. "We were going to have dinner tonight, but Ruby suggested girls' night, and I guess I used it as an excuse to postpone things."

"No harm in that," Elle said. "Besides, I think we all needed this tonight."

"We did." Ruby tugged at her ever-present bun. "Although in the interest of full disclosure, I also wanted to tell you something I'd heard about Jake."

"If it's any kind of scandalous gossip, I don't believe a word of it." After last night, Megan had no doubt Jake was a gentleman through and through. Not many men would remain faithful to a comatose wife for almost a decade, and it told her everything she needed to know about him, as far as she was concerned.

"Not scandalous at all," Ruby said. "Just…information. And since you're considering a relationship with him, it feels weird for me to know it and not tell you."

Megan sipped from her wine. "Spill, then."

"Apparently, Jake's wife came from a very strict, religious family. She was saving herself for marriage."

"Okay," Megan said, not really understanding what this had to do with Jake.

"They started dating when they were fifteen." Ruby raised her eyebrows for emphasis. "She fell during the reception, which means they never consummated their marriage."

"Oh shit," Megan whispered.

Elle slapped a hand over her mouth.

"Which means, either Jake hasn't had sex since he was fifteen," Ruby said, "or if you believe the rumors, he's still a virgin."

## 8

"*A* virgin?" Megan's wine sloshed over the side of the glass as she raised it to her lips and gulped. "That's ridiculous. No way."

"It's not ridiculous at all," Ruby said, "given his situation."

"That poor man," Elle said quietly.

"Oh God." Megan took another gulp from her wine, remembering the awed look on Jake's face when he'd held her last night. Was it possible he'd never held a woman before? Surely, he and Alana had at least fooled around.

"It's not a bad thing," Ruby said. "I mean, if anything, it's honorable."

"Should I feel weird about this?" Megan speared a bite of chicken. "I mean, I'm pretty much the opposite of a virgin. And I've never had sex with one before either."

"Not at all," Ruby said. "It's really not a big deal. It's just a rumor I heard, and it felt weird for me not to tell you."

"How do you have all this town gossip that we don't?" Elle asked her. "You never go out without us. In fact, I can't remember the last time you went out at all."

Ruby was suddenly very interested in her dinner, cutting

her chicken with meticulous precision, eyes narrowed behind her glasses.

"Elle's right," Megan said. "What's the deal?"

Ruby glanced guiltily toward her laptop, which sat on the table beside her bed.

"Have you been checking up on Jake on the internet?" Megan asked.

"Like you did with Theo?" Elle added.

"Not exactly." Ruby looked up at them and sighed. "Okay, I've been hanging out in this online group of local gamers."

"That sounds like you," Elle said with a grin.

"We play online together," Ruby said with a shrug. "They get together once a week to play in person, but I haven't gone yet. I've usually been too busy here at the castle."

"You should totally go," Megan told her. "I'll cover for you if anything needs covering. You need to get out more, Ruby, and these sound like your people."

"Okay, okay," Ruby said, "but anyway, a couple of the women in the group have crushes on Jake. One of them was a good friend of Alana's in high school, so she told us the rumors about his virginity."

"So, nerds are gossips," Elle said with a smile. "Who knew?"

"We can be huge gossips," Ruby said. "And everyone would know that if you bothered to pay attention."

"What are you going to do, Megan?" Elle asked.

"I don't know," she answered honestly. This was exactly why she'd decided not to date this year. She needed to sort herself out before she got involved with anyone else. But could she really walk away from Jake without exploring the chemistry between them?

"I think you should do whatever feels right," Ruby said.

"That's one of those things that sounds so simple," Megan said, sipping from her wine. "But how do I know I'm not just letting my hormones cloud my better judgment?"

"Well, what's the worst that can happen?" Elle asked.

Megan contemplated this for a minute. "Jake realizes he's not ready, or the sex is terrible and we still have to see each other around the castle every day, or we have great sex but things get awkward between us somehow, and again...we're stuck working on the same property."

"I don't think the sex will be terrible," Ruby said, grinning into her wine. "And there's no reason you have to go down to the barn if things get awkward between you two. The rescue horses will be gone soon enough, and then Jake's on his own from us, more or less."

"Plus, you've always been good at staying civil with your exes in the past," Elle added.

*But this is different*, Megan wanted to say. Jake was already more to her than a random man she'd picked up in a bar, and she was still in an emotionally vulnerable place after the accident. But maybe a few passionate nights with Jake could help her heal. "I guess I'll just see what happens when we have dinner tomorrow night."

JAKE WANDERED the aisles of the local supermarket, consulting the list of ingredients he needed to cook dinner for Megan tonight. Maybe it was ambitious, cooking for her instead of taking her out, but the things they needed to discuss weren't things he wanted an audience for.

He wasn't sure whether they ought to pursue a relationship. It certainly wasn't ideal, given that they both lived and worked on the castle grounds—close quarters if things didn't work out. But there was no denying the chemistry crackling between them either.

He turned down the toiletry aisle to grab a new bottle of shampoo when the condom display caught his eye. Should he…? He scraped a hand over his chin, glancing surreptitiously up and down the aisle. There was absolutely no reason for him to feel self-conscious about buying condoms, and yet…small town and all. If he was spotted buying condoms, half the population of Towering Pines would know about it in no time. Better not.

But what if things went well between him and Megan tonight? He reached for a box. *Ribbed for her pleasure*, it announced in big, purple letters. He faltered. Magnum. Ultra. Flavored. Colored. Lubricated. There were dozens of different kinds, and he was painfully aware that he'd never bought condoms before.

It felt almost ludicrous for him to be standing here now, in front of the condom display at the grocery store on a random Sunday afternoon. So what if he and Megan had kissed a couple of times now? That didn't necessarily mean they would take things farther.

But it was better to be prepared than not, and even if he didn't have sex with Megan, he was a single man, had been widowed for almost a year, and sooner or later, he was going to have to climb into this particular saddle. Hopefully sooner than later, if his dick had any say in the matter.

He grabbed a nondescript black box and shoved it below the rest of his groceries, continuing down the aisle with what he hoped was casual nonchalance.

"Jake?"

He turned at the sound of his mother-in-law's voice. Tina Robertson was walking toward him, a wide smile on her face, pushing a cart of her own. "Hi, Tina."

"Fancy seeing you here," she said. "How are things going at the castle so far?"

"Really well," he told her.

"Have you already started training that new horse for Mr. Nichols?"

He nodded. "Duchess. Gorgeous thing. She'll make a wonderful horse for Kassie."

"I have no doubt, especially with you training her." Her gaze dropped to the contents of his cart, and his face turned flaming hot. A package of steaks sat on top, next to a container of baking chocolate and a bottle of red wine. He might as well have written "date" at the top of his shopping list and stuck it to the cart. "Are you cooking dinner for someone?" she asked, her tone rising slightly.

Jake cleared his throat awkwardly. "Having a friend over for dinner, yeah."

She looked up at him with sad eyes. "It's been almost a year, Jake. It's natural that you'll want to date other women. Alana would want that for you."

"It's just dinner, Tina. I'm not sure I'm ready for more than that yet." The bottle of wine rolled to the side, and the corner of the box of condoms peeked out from beneath a head of lettuce. Jake felt like his face must be redder than the wine.

"Take your time, dear, and do what feels right," she said, oblivious, as she touched his arm gently.

"I will." He silently prayed that she wouldn't look inside his cart again, that she wouldn't recognize the box for what it was. After all, the Robertsons were so devoutly religious that Alana had been willing to wait until her wedding night to lose her virginity. If Tina saw the box of condoms, she would be disappointed in him, and that feeling sat like a boulder in his gut.

"Well, I won't keep you," she said, abandoning her cart to give him a spontaneous hug. "Speaking of dinner, it's been too long since we've had you at our table. Could you make it for supper on Wednesday? I could make that roast you like so much."

"I'd like that a lot, Tina. Thank you."

His cheeks were still flaming hot as she turned the corner. He almost grabbed the box of condoms from his cart and put it back on the shelf, but that would be ridiculous. He was a grown-ass man who had a date tonight, a date with a woman who made him hotter than he could ever remember feeling, and he wasn't going to apologize for it or deny himself this opportunity to move forward with his life.

He finished his shopping and brought the cart to a checkout lane manned by a teenage boy he'd never seen before. The kid rang him up without comment—or recognition—and Jake made it out to his truck without further embarrassment.

At home, he put everything away and pulled up the recipe on his phone that he'd found earlier for chocolate fondue. He just had to make the sauce and put out a plate of stuff for them to dip in it. Sounded easy...and romantic. The only problem was that he couldn't make it ahead of time. He'd have to melt the chocolate and serve it after supper.

Well, no problem. He might need an activity to keep his hands occupied after they ate. A burst of nerves fired through him. He was so out of practice, so inexperienced.

Dinner. It was just dinner.

To settle his mind, he went down to the barn and saddled Twister. They went for a long ride on the trails adjacent to the castle, breaking into a canter in the open field just over the hill. With the wind whipping in his face and the pounding of Twister's hooves against the dirt obliterating everything else from his consciousness, Jake finally relaxed. He melted into the saddle, one with the beast beneath him.

After his ride, he took a long shower, shaved, and dressed in a fresh pair of jeans and a black T-shirt. Nothing too fancy. Just dinner. He prepped their salad and rubbed seasoning on the steaks. Didn't think about the box of condoms in the table beside his bed.

There was a knock at the door.

Everything inside him went all warm and tight. He rubbed his hands against his jeans, took a deep breath, and opened the door. Megan stood there wearing formfitting jeans, a dark green top, and a smile that knocked the knees right out from under him.

~

Megan stood on Jake's doorstep, inexplicably breathless at the sight of him. "Hi."

"Hey." His eyes melted her from the inside out, his gaze locked on hers as he motioned for her to come inside. "I hope you like steaks?"

She nodded. "That sounds great."

"I didn't know," he paused, giving her a hesitant glance, "so I made sure everything I bought was Kosher."

She pressed a hand against her chest. "I'm not very strict with it, but it really means a lot to me that you even thought to check. Thank you." Most men never did. In fact, she wasn't sure she'd ever dated anyone who had, unless he was Jewish too. But, as she was learning, Jake wasn't most men.

He nodded, cracking one of those smiles that revealed the dimple in his right cheek. "Wouldn't make a very good impression if I cooked you a meal you couldn't eat, would it?"

"Very thoughtful of you." She stepped closer, sliding her fingers over the kitchen counter. "What would you have done if I was a vegetarian?"

"Uh." He gave her a blank look, as if this had never crossed his mind. "I reckon we would have put the steaks back in the fridge and gone out to dinner."

Dammit, she liked him more and more with every word out of his mouth. "Good answer, but I have to say…I'm really looking forward to having you cook for me tonight."

"I'm glad." He looked genuinely pleased by this.

She leaned against the counter. "Anything I can help with?"

"Nope. The steaks are already on the grill, so we're in good shape. Wine?" He gestured toward a bottle on the counter.

"Sure." She watched as he opened it and poured two glasses. "Thank you."

"Bug's still looking good," he said, raising his glass for a sip. "Checked on her when I took Twister for a ride earlier."

"I stopped in to visit her before I knocked on your door," she admitted.

"I see where your priorities are." There was a teasing glint in his eye.

They kept the easy conversation going while Jake set out their salads, and together they sat at the table to eat. By the time she'd finished her salad, he'd brought in the steaks, which he served with roasted red potatoes.

"This is really good," she told him after she'd taken a bite of the steak. "I have to admit, I didn't expect you to be able to cook."

"If a man lives alone long enough, he learns how to cook the basics. It was that or let my in-laws invite me to dinner every night, and while I do love them, I don't need to spend that much time with them."

"It must have been awkward, living on their property for so long," she said.

"Not awkward exactly." He looked thoughtful. "But…if I say suffocating, that sounds even worse, doesn't it? It was time for me to move out and move on."

"I think that's totally fair," she agreed. "And I'm glad things worked out with the barn and farmhouse here at the castle."

"So am I." He looked up, and their gazes caught. "Although it definitely complicates the things I'm feeling for you."

"It doesn't have to." She tipped her head, watching as he took a sip of his wine. "I've dated enough guys to know I'm good at being civil after things end. It wouldn't have to make our positions here at the castle awkward."

"That's good to know…I think." He gave her an amused glance.

She rolled her eyes. "I'm just saying, I don't tend to attract drama in my relationships. We could stay friends and be professional to each other afterward, if we got far enough into a relationship to warrant a breakup."

"Okay." He looked a little bit uncomfortable with the shift in the conversation.

"This is what we planned dinner to discuss, right?" she said. "How things would work between us if we decided to take things farther?"

"Yes." He nodded, standing to clear away their plates. "You're right."

"I'm not looking for anything serious right now," she said as she picked up her wine and followed him into the kitchen. "I'm focused on my photography and the stuff we've got going on here at the castle. And I'm assuming you're not either. I mean, you're just getting back into the dating game."

"Yeah." Something heavy shimmered in his eyes.

"Which is not to say we should do this," she added, because it needed to be said, for both of their sake. "Just because we're attracted to each other doesn't mean we have to act on it."

"I'm not so sure we're capable of behaving ourselves." His tone dropped, low and gritty and sexy as hell. "Are you?"

"No," she answered, breathless. "But we can be friends who sometimes kiss…if that's what you want."

"It's not what I want."

A warm ache grew between her thighs. "Yeah, me neither."

"Dessert?" he asked, his eyes blown with lust, and she had no idea what they were talking about at this point. Food or sex? Her answer was the same either way.

"Yes."

He walked toward the stove, and she held in her disappointment that he was going to have to make whatever it was, because she was as hungry to touch him as she was for dessert. He set a pot on the stove and filled it with baking chocolate, milk, and butter, stirring until it became a thick sauce. The kitchen filled with the sweet, pungent scent of chocolate.

"Fondue," he said as he poured it into a bowl and placed it between them with a platter of fruit and cookies for dipping.

Okay, so maybe this wasn't a bad idea after all. "Holy shit, that looks good."

"Doesn't it?" He reached for a strawberry, dipped it in the chocolate, and held it toward her lips.

She took a bite, moaning as the cold, tart flavor of the strawberry combined with the hot, rich chocolate on her tongue. "Perfect," she said once she'd swallowed. Delicious and also sexy. Jake was better at this than he knew.

She dipped a bite-sized cookie and popped it in his mouth, leaning in to kiss away the chocolate on his lips. Before she knew it, her back was against the counter and Jake's hands were on her waist, his tongue in her mouth.

"Even better," she murmured.

He reached for another strawberry, feeding it to her as his lips wandered over her neck to the pendant dangling between her breasts. He pushed it aside and kissed the skin there, his lips hot and demanding.

"I think I like this dessert even better," he said as his lips continued their exploration.

"Me too," she gasped, her hips swaying forward, seeking his.

He straightened, bringing their bodies into alignment, the hard ridge of his cock pressed between her legs. Then, he swiped his finger through the fondue and brought it to her mouth. She sucked, and his hips jerked, a string of swears tumbling from his lips. He dipped his head, kissing her deep and thorough, their tongues dancing together through the cocktail of fruit and chocolate on their lips.

"You feel so good," he murmured between kisses, his hips moving rhythmically against hers.

"Mm." She closed her eyes, absorbing every sensation, the way her skin tingled beneath his touch and the heat building between her legs with every movement of their bodies.

"Megan." He stilled, dropping his head to her neck, pressing gentle kisses there as he panted for breath. "There's something else I need to tell you before we take this any farther."

Her eyes popped open. "Okay."

"I told you I hadn't been with anyone since my wife," he said, his expression serious. "But that isn't the whole story."

She nodded, her throat gone dry.

"It was important to Alana to wait for our wedding night," he said. "Her family's very religious. So, we never had sex."

"I'm sorry," she whispered. "And before Alana?"

"We started dating when we were fifteen," he said quietly. "I was a virgin then, and...I still am."

She blinked and shook her head, a wave of emotion barreling up her throat. "That's...I'm not sure what to say."

"It is what it is," he said with a shrug. "I certainly never meant for it to happen."

She wiped away the tears that had slipped over her cheeks, confused and somewhat embarrassed by her reaction to his confession. "So, *you* aren't opposed to premarital sex, then?"

"Hell, no." He gripped her hips, pulling her flush against him. "I am very in favor of it, especially right now."

She put her hands on his chest, pushing him far enough back to meet his eyes. "I've been with a lot of guys, Jake. I'm not apologizing for it, but I understand if that makes you uncomfortable, considering."

He cupped her face, drawing her in for a tender kiss. "On the contrary, I think it's good that one of us knows what they're doing."

Relief rushed through her, loosening her limbs so that she was once again pressed against him. "So, did you guys fool around or anything?"

"Oh yeah. We fooled around a *lot*." He huffed with mirthless laughter. "We did everything you could do without having to call it sex."

Well, that was a relief. Somehow, knowing that he wasn't completely inexperienced made her feel better about the situation. Then they were kissing again, mouths meeting messily as hands groped and hips sought friction. Jake's hands slid beneath her top, and the roughened pads of his fingers felt like heaven against her skin.

"So soft," he said as he slid up her back. "Can't get enough."

Neither could she. Her fingers hooked under the hem of his T-shirt, lifting it over his head. He briefly withdrew his hands from her body to untangle himself from the shirt, and holy hell, his chest was a thing of wonder, lean and muscular from countless hours working in the barn, somehow impossibly sexier than muscles gained at the gym.

The front of his jeans strained to contain his cock. She pressed a palm against his length, as intimidated as she was turned on by the knowledge of his virginity. He groaned, pressing his hips more firmly into her touch, and she gripped him through the denim, giving him a firm squeeze.

"Fuck," he hissed, his hands shaking as they returned to her waist. "I, ah, I may have a slight problem."

"What's that?" She withdrew her hand, meeting his eyes.

His face was strained, tension vibrating through every inch of his body. "I want this more than anything, but—"

She took a step back, heart thudding in her chest, desire mixing with disappointment. "It's okay. We don't have to do anything else, not tonight anyway."

"Will you let me finish?" He tugged her against him. "The problem is that I want it *too* much. It's been too long, Meg. I can't…I can't wait."

"Oh," she whispered as the ache inside her intensified, the desperation in his eyes burning right through her. "*Oh.*"

"I want to go slow. I want to do this right. I'm embarrassing myself."

"Don't be," she murmured, reaching down to unzip his jeans. "It's incredibly hot to see you this turned on."

"You're going to be the death of me," he gritted as she palmed him through his boxer briefs.

"What you need is a pressure release so you can slow down and enjoy the rest of our evening." She pushed down his underwear, and his cock jutted between them, thick and hard, a bead of moisture already glistening at the tip. She dropped to her knees, licking it off, her eyes never leaving his.

He let out a rough sound, his cock jumping against her lips.

"This is a beautiful cock," she murmured, running her hand up and down his length. "And it's waited so patiently for all these years."

"I don't know about patiently." Jake's voice had gone impossibly deep and rough.

"A perfect gentleman," she said before swirling her tongue over his head. She pushed him backward until his ass rested against the counter, and then she took him in deep, sucking him all the way to the back of her throat in one movement.

"Fuck me," he gritted, hips jerking as he attempted to hold himself back. She gripped his ass, encouraging him to thrust into her mouth, adjusting the angle of her head to take him in. His legs shook, fingers tangled in the depths of her hair as he let out a groan.

She swirled her tongue around him and sucked, hard. His hips jerked again, beginning to move, settling into a rhythm of quick thrusts as a string of curses left his lips.

"I'm going to come," he rasped, hips moving faster and faster.

She sucked harder, letting her tongue cushion him, sliding over the vein that ran along the underside of his cock.

"Fuck," he shouted as the first spurt hit her tongue. "Oh God, fuck, oh...oh...yes."

He kept coming, and she kept sucking, swallowing his release, pressing her thighs together against the desire pulsing in her core. She was ridiculously turned on by getting him off. The expression on his face was quite possibly the most erotic thing she'd ever seen, a mixture of desperation and ecstasy and relief.

Finally, his hips stilled, his muscles going slack. He slid out of her mouth, pulling her against him as his knees buckled and he sank to the kitchen floor, taking her with him.

"Goddamn, woman." He held her tight, his chest heaving against hers, his whole body shaking in the aftermath of his release. "I don't know how I survived ten years without that."

"I don't either," she answered as she tucked him back into his jeans and zipped him up. "There. Now we can slow down and enjoy ourselves."

"Not until I've evened the playing field," he said, drawing her into his lap. "If I hadn't been so damn desperate, I had planned to take care of you first."

"I do appreciate a man with a 'ladies' first' policy," she said as she dipped her head to kiss him. "But in this situation, you definitely deserved to cut the line."

"I'll make it up to you," he murmured into her mouth, his fingers working at the button of her jeans. "Repeatedly."

"No objections." Her breath caught as his hand slid inside her jeans, cupping her through her panties.

"You're so wet for me." There was a hint of wonder in his voice, reminding her of the reality of his situation, although she was relieved to know this wasn't the first time he'd touched a woman.

She squirmed against him as he pushed her panties to the side. The position was awkward, but he lifted her up slightly in his lap, maximizing his leverage as the pad of his thumb scraped over her clit, sending her mind whirling. He stroked her, building a rhythm with his fingers, and holy shit, that blow job had really done a number on her, because she was already climbing toward release, her body throbbing beneath his touch.

He shifted, pushing first one, then a second big, strong finger inside her, and she cried out in relief, rocking in his lap as he took her right over the edge. Release pulsed through her, leaving her panting in his arms.

"Beautiful," he whispered, bringing his mouth to hers for a

kiss. He slid his hand out of her jeans, and she straddled him, deepening the kiss, not entirely surprised to feel him already semi-hard inside his jeans. He had a lot of lost time to make up for. And if their warm-up session was any indication, she was going to enjoy every minute.

## 9

ake swallowed the bite of cake dipped in chocolate that Megan held against his lips, hunger and desire mixing in his veins. It had hardly been half an hour since he'd come, and already, he was rock hard again inside his jeans. He had a feeling he might be hard forever when he was near her. Maybe this intense feeling of need would never go away.

Or maybe it would ease once he'd been inside her.

Goddamn, his mind almost exploded at the thought. He drew her against him, arms wrapped around her, kissing her deeply and thoroughly. "Never get tired of this," he murmured against her mouth.

"Me neither." The smile she gave him did funny things inside his chest.

"What do you say we move this to the bedroom?" he asked, hoping he sounded more nonchalant than he felt.

"Lead the way." Her voice was equal parts sex and affection.

He slid his hand into hers as they walked down the hall. In the bedroom, he switched on the little lamp by the bed so they wouldn't be fumbling in the dark, leaving the overhead light off to help set the mood. Not that they seemed to need any help setting the mood. The only help he might need was making it through the next few minutes without coming in his pants.

Then again, that was probably his virginity talking.

They stood beside the bed, bodies pressed together, kissing, somehow both still fully dressed, except for his shirt, which was left behind in the kitchen. He slipped his hands beneath her top, skimming it up her sides, his fingers tracing her skin as he went. She lifted her arms, and he tossed it to the floor, revealing the black lace bra she wore beneath.

"Sexy." He traced his fingers over the lace, feeling her nipples harden beneath his touch. He cupped her breasts, enjoying the feel of them in his hands, the weight of them against his palms, so warm and full beneath the lace.

Megan let out a sigh, her head falling back as he touched her. He slid his hands down her stomach to the waistband of her jeans before unzipping them and pushing them down her legs. She kicked them off, revealing a matching black lace thong beneath.

"Goddamn." His voice had gone hoarse. "You're so beautiful."

"You're not half bad to look at yourself," she said as she unbuttoned his jeans. "Sure you're ready for this?"

"Never been more sure of anything in my life." He pressed his hips against hers, letting her feel just how ready he was.

"Then I think you've waited long enough."

He stepped out of his jeans and underwear and pulled her close, her bare skin against his, a sensation so intense it was almost overwhelming. He thrust against her, letting the lace of her thong scrape against the sensitive head of his cock, completely lost to the thrill of it.

"The look on your face when you touch me is one of the sexiest things I've ever seen," she murmured, her hands on his ass, urging him on.

"That's because touching you is the sexiest thing I've experienced in a long damn time."

Megan reached behind herself, unclasping her bra and tossing it to the floor. Her breasts bounced free, nipples already hardened into tight peaks, and he dipped his head, drawing first one and then the other into his mouth, swirling his tongue over her sensitive skin, thrilled with the needy sounds that escaped her lips.

He pushed down her panties, taking a moment to appreciate her beauty before he wrapped his arms around her, kissing her while their bodies pressed together, his cock nestled against the warm, bare skin of her belly, throbbing with the most beautifully intense sense of anticipation. "Finally," he whispered.

"You could say that." She reached between them and gripped him, sending a bolt of fire through him so powerful he thought he might come right there in her hand.

"I think it's better if I do the touching for now," he said, removing her hand.

"Well, that's no fun...for you at least." She gave him a wicked grin.

"Holding on to my control by a thread here," he told her. "I need to make sure you're as close as I am before I'm inside you or I won't be able to last long enough for you to join me."

"Fair enough." Her voice had taken on a breathless quality.

He pushed her onto the bed, his body covering hers, bare skin touching bare skin. "Do you have any idea how many times I've fantasized about this?"

She gasped as he slipped a hand between her legs to stroke her. "About sex, or about me?"

"Both, but mostly you. I tried not to think about sex while I was still married, since it wasn't an option for me. But since I met you...I can't stop fantasizing about you, Megan. You're all I can think about."

"Oh," she murmured, her hips moving rhythmically against his hand.

He pressed himself against her, so hard it hurt and so happy he felt like he might burst from it...or maybe it was his cock that was about to burst.

"Tell me when you're close," he whispered, rubbing his thumb against her clit, thrilled by the wetness coating his fingers, the evidence of her arousal.

"Getting there." Her hips moved faster, pressing against his hand.

He dipped his head and kissed her, drinking her in, letting their bodies move together as the heat between them blazed.

"Close," she whispered, hips jerking against his hand. "Hurry."

"Happy to." He sat up, reaching for the box of condoms he'd left in the table by the bed earlier.

"Did you buy those just for me?" she asked, chest heaving, cheeks flushed, watching him through glazed eyes.

"Sure did." He ripped it open and pulled out a little foil packet. "Don't laugh if I fuck this up."

"I would never," she said, her voice low and throaty. "Make sure you leave room at the tip."

"Got it." He positioned the condom and rolled it on, relieved to get it right on the first try.

"You're a natural," she said, laying back on the bed.

"I hope so." He held himself above her, body taut and trembling, almost overcome in anticipation.

"I'll be gentle with you," she whispered.

"Baby, I don't want gentle." He lowered his hips, and his cock brushed against her. His eyes almost rolled back his head at that simple contact. He hoped he didn't embarrass himself by coming before he even got inside her. But, after twenty-eight years of anticipation, he supposed he was entitled to be in a hurry. Carefully, he guided himself to her entrance, pausing there to meet her eyes, making sure she was ready.

"The moment you've been waiting for." She grinned up at him, her eyes gleaming in the reflection of the lamp.

"Oh yeah." He pushed slowly inside, groaning the whole

way. It was impossibly better than he'd imagined, the feel of her hot and tight around him, gripping him from base to tip. "Fuuuuuck."

"Good?" she panted, arching her back so that their chests pressed together.

"Good is such an inadequate word." He withdrew and plunged back in, sending shockwaves of sensation through his body. And then he was pounding into her, hard and fast, completely overwhelmed by the need burning up his spine, filling his balls and tingling its way into his cock. Frantic, he reached between them and began to stroke her, desperate to make sure he didn't run off and leave her at the finish line.

"Oh God," she moaned, moving beneath him, her tits bouncing with every thrust of his body into hers.

"Yes, yes, oh fuck, yes." He heard the words coming out of his mouth, and then Megan's body clamped down on him, a sharp cry echoing on her lips as she started to come, taking him with her. "Oh yeah, baby, that's it...yesssssss." He groaned as release tore through him in hot waves that seemed to shake him from head to foot. His hips bucked against her as he came.

Afterward, he dropped to the bed beside her, one arm thrown over his face, his whole body limp and shaking.

"So, what did you think?" Megan asked, amusement lacing her tone.

"Sorry, can't talk because my brain just exploded."

She laughed, soft and throaty. "I thought that was a different part of your anatomy."

"Yeah, that too." He rolled toward her, brushing away a lock of silky brown hair. "All kidding aside, that was amazing, and not just because it was my first time."

She blinked, her eyes looking suspiciously glossy for a moment. "I think it was mostly because it was your first time."

"Maybe." He sat up, removing the condom. He carried it to the trash in the bathroom before returning to the bed. He lifted the sheet as he climbed back in, inviting her to join him under the covers. They rolled together, arms and legs entwined.

"So, do you feel different?" she asked, still with a teasing light in her eyes.

"Just relieved, mostly. It was messing with my head, wondering when and if I'd ever get to do this thing everyone else in the world seemed to be doing…and enjoying."

"Yeah, I can see that." Her voice was soft, pillowed by the blankets around them.

He closed his eyes for a moment, content to feel the warmth of her skin and the puff of her breath against his neck, thinking that he could hold her forever and never get tired of it. "Officially not even in the same ballpark as jerking off."

"Especially when I call in the middle and interrupt you?" she whispered.

"Especially then, although I let you interrupt me," he told her. "I didn't have to answer the phone. I guess I just wanted to hear your voice before I came."

"Well, that's hot. Feel free to call when you're horny any time."

"I think that sounds like an excellent idea." He ran his hands down her back, still mesmerized by the freedom to touch her, the comfort he felt at the closeness of their bodies. "It feels so good to hold you."

"Just hold me?" She pressed herself against his cock, which was already hard again.

"I can't help it. I have a lot of time to make up on," he said with a smile. "But I really do enjoy holding you. Will you stay? I'd love to sleep next to you."

"Yeah, I'll stay." She smiled up at him, something tender, almost tentative on her face. "I already asked Elle to watch my foster dogs tonight, just in case. God knows I watched hers enough times when she and Theo were first dating."

"Good." He fingered the silver pendant on her chest, the one she always wore. "Does it have special meaning for you?"

"Well, it's the Tree of Life, which has a lot of really cool meanings, but also it was a gift from my grandmother." Her fingers brushed over his to touch the pendant.

They lay together for a few minutes of peaceful silence, just enjoying the closeness between them. His fingers encountered the scar on her arm, and he traced it idly, running his thumb over it like a map to her body. She shivered, pulling away. "Sorry. Does it hurt?"

She shook her head.

"Lord knows I have enough of them." He lifted his arm, showing her the scar on his elbow where a horse had thrown him when he was sixteen. He'd caught it on the fence as he fell, needed several dozen stitches to close it back up. "Gives us character, right?" He cupped her cheek, not quite touching the scar there.

She turned her face against the pillow.

"Hey. You okay?"

"Fine." But something in her tone had gone taut, her face still turned so that the pillow hid her scar.

He felt a tug deep in his chest, somewhere in the vicinity of his heart. He barely even noticed the scars when he looked at her, had never really stopped to think how she might feel about them. He supposed he'd just assumed she didn't notice them any more than he did. In retrospect, that had been a stupid thing to assume. After all, he'd seen the way she sometimes wore her hair over her face, hiding behind it.

"I'm sorry," he said softly, although he wasn't quite sure what he was apologizing for.

Megan's gaze drifted toward the ceiling, her expression carefully blank.

"In my eyes, it only makes you more beautiful."

She sat up, and there it was, that curtain of hair falling over her face. She made no effort to brush it away as she slid out of bed and walked into the bathroom, closing the door firmly behind her.

MEGAN STOOD at the bathroom sink, glaring at herself in the mirror. This was meant to be a special night for Jake, and she was ruining it. She blew out a deep, cleansing breath before bending to splash cold water over her face. She closed her eyes as she patted her skin dry on the hand towel.

Moments like these, the scar was all she could see. It throbbed beneath the heat of her own gaze, seeming to redden from her shame. She had the irrational urge to claw at it, as though she could rip it off her face, be rid of it, be herself again.

But that was ridiculous. Her scars didn't define her. At least, they shouldn't. It was only her own foolish vanity that gave them power. So, why couldn't she seem to reclaim that power for herself?

She needed to get a grip, like, *right now*.

And then she needed to get back out there and salvage this night, because Jake absolutely did not deserve her bullshit tonight or any other night. The man had suffered enough. He'd watched his wife die for nine years, and here she was being a drama queen about the scars on her face.

She gave herself one final glare in the mirror, fingers clenched around the edge of the counter, before walking back into the bedroom. Jake lay right where she'd left him, sprawled naked and handsome across the bed, his eyes locked on hers.

"You okay?" he asked as she slid in beside him, draping an arm across his stomach.

"Yes."

"Sorry if I said something wrong." His gaze was still locked on hers, steady and intense.

"You didn't." She moved to kiss him, but he stopped her with a gentle hand cupping her chin, holding her gaze, unsatisfied with her answer. She sighed, dropping her face into his hand. "I get self-conscious about it sometimes. It's stupid. I know it is."

"It's not stupid," he told her earnestly. "If anything's stupid, it's the importance our society puts on the perfection of our faces, or bodies in general. Animals don't fall for any of that superficial bullshit."

"We'd do well to be more like them," she said quietly.

"They have a lot more common sense than we do sometimes," he said with a teasing smile before his expression turned serious. "You know I mean it when I say I don't even notice your scars most of the time. They're just a part of your face, no better or worse than any other part."

"Thank you." She turned her face to kiss his palm, her skin flushing hot at his words, even as her heart recognized his honesty. She made a point to tuck her hair behind her ear before she brought her lips to his. *See, I'm fine.*

But deep down she knew he could see right through her.

## 10

------------

Jake woke slowly, wonderfully aware of the warm presence beside him. Bone deep satisfaction lingered like a drug in his system. He opened his eyes to see Megan sprawled across the bed on her stomach, one arm thrust in his direction, legs tangled in the sheets. He grinned, reaching out to run his fingers through the wild tangle of her hair. She let out a sleepy sigh, rolling toward him.

"Morning," he said, his voice deep and raspy with sleep.

"Mm," she mumbled, squinting at him. "What time is it?"

"No idea. Around six, if I had to guess." His internal clock was pretty accurate, a result of years of getting up and getting his ass to the barn first thing in the morning.

Megan scooted closer, eyes sliding shut as she draped herself against his chest. "I should go soon to help with breakfast at the castle."

"You don't look like you want to go anywhere." He wrapped an arm around her, thinking how great it was to wake next to someone, to start his morning with a kiss, a warm body pressed against his, the comforting presence of another person, especially *this* person. Of all the things he'd discovered in the last twelve hours, sleeping—actually *sleeping*—with Megan was pretty damn high on the list.

Her hips brushed against his beneath the sheets, and her fist wrapped around his cock. Then she was peering up at him, looking decidedly more awake. "Someone's happy to see me this morning."

"Pretty curious to see what all the fuss about morning sex is about," he told her. "Care to indulge me?"

"I could probably be persuaded."

"Oh yeah?" He leaned in to kiss her, slow and deep. "Is this persuasive enough?"

"Not quite," she whispered, a grin tugging at her lips.

"I can be very persuasive when I need to be." He dipped his head, bringing his mouth to her breast. He grazed his teeth against the sensitive flesh there before sucking her nipple into his mouth, teasing it with his tongue.

Megan sighed with pleasure, melting closer against him under the covers. "Almost convinced."

He transferred his attention to the other breast while sliding one of his hands between her legs, stroking through the wetness he found there. Her body was a marvel to him, and he wanted to explore every inch, to discover everything she enjoyed and all the different ways to make her come. He had so much to learn.

"Okay, yeah, I'm convinced," she panted.

He reached for a condom and rolled it on, more confidently this time. Last night, things had been fumbled and fast, a rush toward release. This morning, he wanted to take his time and savor the moment. He pushed slowly inside her, groaning all the way. "Still can't believe how good this feels."

"Mm," she mumbled, arching her back beneath him.

He held still for a long moment, just feeling her tight heat gripping him, the way his cock pulsed with anticipation. Desire rippled through him, hot and urgent, heightening his senses. He leaned forward and captured her mouth as he began to move, stroking leisurely. "Could get used to waking up every morning this way."

She smiled against his lips.

They kissed, rocking together in a perfect sort of rhythm. He kept the pace slow for as long as he could, letting the heat between them build before he finally started to lose control, his hips bucking faster against hers. Megan was right there with him, meeting each of his thrusts with one of her own, bringing their bodies together just right.

"I'm close," he panted.

"Go on," she whispered, eyes sliding shut. Her body gripped his as she started to come.

"Oh yeah," he gritted as his own orgasm took hold. "Fuck yes." He held himself still as release poured through him before rolling onto the bed beside her. "Definitely a good morning now."

She smiled, eyes still closed, a blissed-out expression on her face.

"Wish I could stay in bed with you all day," he said.

"Someone has sex on the brain," she whispered, pressing a kiss against his neck.

"Can't help it."

They lay together for a few minutes, while they caught their breath, and Jake felt an unfamiliar sort of peace come over him. It had been a good night, a good morning, and he had no reason to expect today wouldn't be a good one too.

Might even end with Megan in his bed again.

He hadn't come to Rosemont Castle looking for a woman. He'd come to establish his career and make a name for himself as a horse trainer. Maybe this thing with Megan would just be a fling, but even so, he couldn't bring himself to regret it. Instead, as he lay there with one arm around her, their legs tangled in the sheets with the morning sun streaming in through the window, he realized it had been a mistake not to seek out this kind of companionship sooner.

Maybe he hadn't been ready before now. Either way, now that he knew what it felt like to sleep beside a woman, to wake with her in his arms and lose himself inside her, he never wanted to be alone again.

They showered together—and he got to experience shower sex for the first time—before Megan dressed and headed to the castle to get ready for her day. Maybe working on the same propterty would be a good thing. They were close enough to drop in on each other at a moment's notice, to easily spend the night together, but still worked far enough apart that they didn't have to see each other if they didn't want to.

He headed to the barn to tend to the horses. Twister trotted across his pasture to greet Jake at the gate, while Duchess looked on from her own pasture. Bug and Dusty were, as usual, in the riding ring. He gave everyone a pat before heading into the barn.

Inside, it smelled like horse, that warm scent that called to mind a lifetime of memories, so many barns, so many animals he'd worked with over the years. And now, it was *his* barn. Not that he owned it, but he had full control over it, and someday, he'd own his own place. In the meantime, this was exactly what he needed.

If only business would pick up, he'd really be in good shape. He'd put out several feelers about his training services since he moved to Rosemont Castle, but so far nothing had panned out. He had enough existing clients to scrape by, but to succeed, he needed more. His budget was stretched to the breaking point right now, but he knew that was the way it went for most new businesses in their first year. For now, he was trying not to worry, especially when everything else in his life seemed to be going so well.

He mucked the stalls that had been used yesterday, cleaned and refilled water buckets, and performed the rest of the morning chores. Once he'd finished, he brought Duchess into the barn and put her on the cross-ties in the aisle for a training session. He spent time grooming and handling her, offering lots of positive reinforcement for her cooperation. To her credit, Duchess was a very cooperative horse.

He put her in her stall while he brought Bug and Dusty inside to free up the riding ring. Then, he got Duchess back out, put the bridle and saddle on her that they'd been using for their training sessions, and brought her out to the arena for some work on the lunge line. He clipped it to her bridle and backed up, allowing her to begin at a walk, looping around him in a circle as they practiced verbal commands.

He spun in a slow circle as she moved, keeping the line from going slack, praising her all the while. Duchess moved with an easy grace, head up, ears pricked, eager to learn and to work. As he turned to face the castle, he saw Megan coming down the lane with her camera in tow. His heart quickened at the sight. She'd changed into dark jeans and a red top, her hair tied back in a loose ponytail.

She came to stand against the fence, watching them. "I saw you out here working with Duchess. Is this a good time for me to take some pictures?"

"Sure." He was grateful that she was taking pictures for him to use on his website and marketing materials, and Duchess was the perfect cover model for his business.

"Pretend I'm not here," she said.

"That's hard to do, when you're all I can think about," he said, only half joking.

"Jake," she admonished, laughter in her tone.

So, he did his best to ignore her, and after a few minutes, he halfway succeeded. He focused on Duchess, working her in both directions before he moved in for some more hands-on direction, asking her to move over and back up for him, getting her comfortable with the commands she'd need to know later on. He walked her up to the mounting block and asked her to stand beside it. Then, he stepped up and put his hands on her back, applying gentle pressure, talking quietly to her the whole time.

She turned her head to stare at him, a "what the hell are you doing?" look on her face, but no signs of discomfort or distress. This horse was as solid as an oak. When he'd finished with her, he brought her into the barn to untack her and praised her with a generous face rub and a few well-earned carrots.

Megan followed, keeping her distance as she photographed him at work. Duchess lifted her head to stare at her, and Megan snapped a series of photos. "My goodness, you're gorgeous," she murmured to the horse, and Duchess nickered in response.

"That she is," Jake said. "Want to give her a treat before I put her back outside?"

"Sure." Megan replaced the camera in its case, slung it over her shoulder, and walked over. She took a baby carrot from Jake's hand and offered it to Duchess with practiced ease. She was one hundred percent more comfortable around the horses these days, and it filled him with an odd sort of pride. And a healthy amount of lust, because watching a woman work with horses had always been a huge turn-on for him.

"I was thinking about taking Twister for a ride. Want to come with me?"

"Come with you, how?" she asked, her brow furrowed.

"On Twister. I wouldn't ask him to do it often, but he could carry us both on a little trail ride. He'd enjoy it, and so would I."

Her eyes lit. "Yeah, that sounds great, actually."

"Got any boots?" he asked, giving Duchess another affectionate rub as he unclipped her from the cross-ties.

"Um, like riding boots?"

"Any boots will do, even cowboy boots," he said with an easy smile, gesturing at his own.

A wide smile split her face. "I do have a pair of those. I bought them after we moved here, and the girls laughed at me.

They accused me of thinking I was in Texas when I asked about going line dancing down at Bar None."

"Yeah, you won't find any line dancing here in Virginia."

"Well, I'm from Florida, so what do I know? But I'll go get my boots and meet you back down here."

"It's a date," he said, leaning in to press a kiss against her lips.

As she walked away, he wondered if he'd ever get used to the ways his life had changed, how good it felt to have her in his bed and in his life. His thoughts drifted to Alana, remembering the many times they'd taken trail rides together, the way Alana's body would sway against his as they rode, the soft brush of her blonde hair over his arms.

They'd thought they had their wholes lives in front of them. He'd lost her, *really* lost her, so long ago, it was usually hard for him to remember, but suddenly he saw her as clearly as if she'd been standing right in front of him, head cocked the way she did when she was teasing him, blue eyes sparkling beneath the hot summer sun. He heard the sound of her laughter, as light as the summer breeze, the slow drawl of her voice when she said his name.

If only she could have been here to see this barn and the things he'd accomplished. He blinked away Alana's image, focusing his eyes on Megan's retreating form, replacing the past with the present. His hands clenched around Duchess's saddle pad as he attempted to anchor himself there.

MEGAN SAT ON HER BED, shoving her feet into the brown leather cowboy boots that had cost way too much to risk getting dirty in the barn, but did she care? Nope. Going for a trail ride with Jake would be worth any amount of dirt on her boots. Their relationship couldn't last. Between the two of them, they had way too much baggage to make it work, but for today, she was having the time of her life, and that was all that mattered.

"What on earth are you doing?" Ruby asked from the doorway. "I thought I had finally convinced you we're in the wrong state for line dancing."

Megan flipped her off with a smile. "For your information, I'm getting ready to go for a ride. On a horse. Which is exactly what these boots are made for."

Ruby raised her eyebrows. "Really? With Jake?"

She nodded as she stood and walked over to Ruby. "These are not as comfortable as they look."

Ruby snorted with laughter. "Are you going to wear a cowboy hat too?"

"You know what? I should. There's got to be one somewhere here in the castle."

"Are we going to talk about what else is going on here?" Ruby asked, not budging from the doorway, eyebrows still lifted for emphasis.

"Like the fact that I spent the night with him?" She lifted her own eyebrows. "I figured you guys had already drawn your own conclusions about that."

"Well, we did," Ruby confirmed with a smile. "But we still want to hear it from you."

"It was an amazing night. And for the record, you were right about him being a virgin," Megan told her, cheeks flushing at the memory. "But he and Alana had fooled around plenty, so he wasn't exactly starting from zero. And he's a quick learner. I'm more than happy to help him make up for lost time."

Ruby's expression softened. "Well, I'm glad it's going well. Elle's off with Theo tonight, but do you want to go into town and get dinner together? If you don't have plans with Jake, that is."

"I definitely can't spend the night with him, because I've got to keep all five of the foster dogs tonight, to make up for Elle watching them for me last night." And she could probably use a little distance from Jake, before this casual thing started to feel...not so casual. "So yeah, let's get dinner."

"Excellent. I'll text later, unless I bump into you in the meantime." With a wave, Ruby headed down the hall toward the room housing their foster cats.

Megan grabbed her jacket and headed for the barn. She found Jake already outside with Twister, silhouetted against the late afternoon sun. If only she'd brought her camera with her, that could have been the cover shot for his website, because damn, they made a handsome pair, the strong man and his equally strong horse. Something about the cowboy hat he wore while riding really did it for her. Actually, everything about him seemed to do it for her.

"Ready?" he called, leading Twister toward the steps so she could climb onto his back.

She nodded as she walked toward them, butterflies of anticipation fluttering in her belly. She'd enjoyed her first ride on Twister, however short, but riding with Jake sounded even more exciting, and especially going out on the trails.

"Just grab ahold of the saddle, like you did last time," Jake instructed. "Put your left foot into the stirrup and swing up onto his back."

She did as he said, hoisting herself up. Twister shifted beneath her, and she gripped him with her thighs to find her balance. There was something amazing about feeling all that strength and power beneath her. "It's the coolest thing," she said. "Being up here on his back."

"Isn't it?" Jake swung into the saddle behind her. "We'll take it nice and easy today, just a relaxing trail ride for all of us."

Jake settled behind her, his chest against her back, as Twister began to walk. It was a disorienting feeling, the sway of the horse beneath her paired with the strong column of Jake's chest behind her. She gripped the horn, feeling like every step of the horse sent her crashing into Jake.

"Relax," he told her. "Just let him move you. You want to stay loose and let your hips take all the movement."

"That sounds like a different kind of activity." She glanced at him over her shoulder.

He gave her a sexy smile. "Could go for either, I guess."

But she did what he said, relaxing her muscles so that her hips swayed with Twister's gait, and soon she found the comfortable rhythm she'd managed last time. She and Jake moved in unison with each step.

"Have you been out on the trails much?" he asked as they approached the edge of the woods that surrounded the castle.

"A few times, probably not as much as I should have. Elle takes the dogs jogging out here a few times a week."

"Twister and I have only been out here a few times too, but we used to ride on trails a lot at our old barn. It's nice. Really peaceful. Plus, you never know when you might surprise a deer or something out here."

"I see why you like it so much." She let herself relax against Jake's chest, looking up at the canopy of trees overhead.

"Riding has always been my escape," he said, his voice rumbling through her. "Nothing better."

They rode in silence for a few minutes. The forest around them was dappled with sunlight as it spilled between the branches of the trees, creating a kaleidoscope of green and gold. She needed to come back out here with her camera too. Why hadn't she photographed the forest before?

The only sound came from the muffled clop of Twister's hooves against the trail, the occasional huff and snort of his breath, and the whisper of the breeze through the trees. Peaceful. Mesmerizing. Combined with the rhythmic movement of the horse beneath her and Jake's warmth pressed up against her back, she felt like she could go into a trance. Maybe this was what it felt like to meditate, heightening your awareness of the world around you.

"Penny for your thoughts," Jake said quietly.

"Just soaking it all in."

"I hear that." He rested a hand on her hip. They came out at a little overlook, the castle and grounds laid out beneath them like something out of a fairytale...or a postcard. The castle itself was impressive, with the tower on one side and the fountain in the middle of the circular drive out front, but add in the gardens off to the left, the barn and pastures and all the other various outbuildings, and it was truly breathtaking.

"Whoa," she whispered. "Sometimes I still can't believe I really get to call this place home."

"Me neither. Big step up for me, that's for sure."

"Where did you grow up?" she asked, realizing she'd never heard him mention his own family, only Alana's.

"A few towns over, in Bakersville."

"And does your family still live there?"

He straightened behind her, not exactly tense, but she still got the distinct impression that she'd touched on an uncomfortable subject for him. "No."

She didn't push, leaning back against him in silent support. Twister tossed his head, picking at a few blades of grass along the trail.

"My mom died when I was seventeen," he said after a pause.

"Oh no. I'm sorry." She reached back to touch him, wishing she could face him, hold him, even see his face.

"Overdose." His tone was low and even, but she could hear the pain behind his words. "She battled addiction my whole life. I barely know my dad. He was never around much, and he lives in Oregon now. I haven't seen him in years. After Mom died, my older sister Helen took a job outside DC. Honestly, the Robertsons have sometimes felt more like family than my own."

She leaned back, pressing her hands against the tops of his thighs. "I really wish I could hug you right now."

His arms slid around her in response. "But I can hug *you*. And it's okay, really. It all happened a long time ago."

"That doesn't mean it doesn't still hurt," she said quietly. Truthfully, she couldn't even imagine what that would be like. She had two awesome parents who loved her and would do anything for her. It made her unspeakably sad to think of Jake basically fending for himself since he was a teenager, or for his whole life, maybe. Growing up with a mother who was an addict couldn't have been easy. Thank God he'd had the Robertsons, at least.

"I really don't think about it that much," he said. "I try to just keep myself in the present."

"That's a good attitude." Honestly, Jake seemed to have handled everything life had thrown at him with an incredible amount of grace. They fell silent for a few minutes, just taking in their surroundings and the closeness between them.

"Do you mind if I ask about your accident?" he asked, his tone gentle.

She forced herself not to straighten, not to pull out of his embrace. "You must have heard about it when it happened."

"I guess I did, but only vaguely."

"We were on our way home from Bar None, Elle, Ruby, and I," she told him. "We'd all been drinking, so we had Theo's driver, James, take us home."

Jake's hand rested on her thigh, warm and comforting.

"A deer ran in front of the car, and James swerved to avoid it." She closed her eyes, remembering the screams, the panic, the pain. "It was a minor accident, really, except a tree branch came through my window."

"I'm sorry," Jake murmured, bending his head to kiss her cheek, right over the scar.

"There was so much blood," she whispered, touching her face reflexively. "It got in my eye, and I thought I was losing my vision, that the branch had gotten my eye too."

"That's a hell of a thing."

"Anyway, tree branches don't make for the neatest wounds,

so…" She would carry the scars from that night on her skin for the rest of her life.

"Nothing neat about it, but life rarely is," he commented, arms still around her, warm and strong.

"I guess not." She relaxed against his chest, shaking off the memories of the crash. "Anyway, I've seen plastic surgeons, done all the creams and treatments, and this is about as good as it's going to get."

He squeezed her leg. "Your scars are part of who you are, and I think everything about you is pretty damn great."

"Thanks." It made sense when he said it, but she hadn't truly felt like herself since the accident. There was Megan from before the crash, and Megan from after. And she wasn't entirely sure who the new Megan was yet. Maybe Jake could help her merge them together. Or maybe she had to do that on her own.

They sat together quietly, watching as the sun inched closer to the treetops, casting the castle and grounds in a golden glow. His arms rested comfortably around her, his hands covering hers on the saddle horn. Beneath them, Twister began to shuffle impatiently.

"Guess we better let him get moving again," she said finally, leaning down to rub the horse's neck.

"Yep." Jake clucked to him, and they were off again, walking down the trail back into the forest. "This trail is a big loop, comes out behind the farmhouse."

"I'm definitely coming back with my camera," she murmured.

"Lots of great shots out here," he agreed.

They rode in an easy silence back to the castle. Jake's arms were still around her, his warm, solid presence pressed against her back, and she could only describe the feeling as…contentment. Which was frankly unsettling in itself. She'd never felt contented with a man before, and it terrified her to feel that way about Jake, when neither of them were in any place to think about a serious relationship.

"So, about tonight…" he said after they'd gotten off Twister and stood together in the barn. There was an awkward moment where they stared at each other, each waiting for the other to make the first move. "I have a late session with an offsite client, and then I really need to catch up on some work. Can I see you tomorrow?"

She exhaled, inexplicably relieved he hadn't been expecting her to spend the night again, because right now she needed a little space to figure out why she felt so…attached after only one night with him. "Definitely, and I promised to have dinner with Ruby tonight anyway."

"All right, then."

"Working on your next book?"

He nodded. "And I'm behind on my word count for this week."

"Well, I'd better let you get to it. Text me about tomorrow, but I'll probably see you around regardless." She leaned in to give him a quick kiss, which turned into a lingering one as his arms slipped around her, anchoring her against his body.

"Not tired of this yet," he murmured against her lips.

"Well, I should hope not," she teased. "It's only been twenty-four hours."

They kissed, slow and lingering until she finally broke away for some much-needed air, forehead resting against his cheek while his chest heaved beneath her palm.

"See you tomorrow, then," she said, stepping backward out of his arms before they got carried away. Because she had no doubt it wouldn't take much for them to get carried away. Not tonight, and not for their relationship in general.

# 11

---

"**S**o where are Elle and Theo tonight anyway?" Megan asked as she twirled pasta around her fork.

Ruby sat across the table from her, dark hair as usual pulled into a messy bun, black-rimmed glasses reflecting the overhead lighting. "They went to a charity event in DC."

"That sounds…stuffy," Megan said with a giggle.

Ruby speared a shrimp out of her seafood linguine with a smile. "Such a chore, schmoozing with rich people. Elle will be in her element, though."

"She will," Megan agreed. "She's good at that. I'd love to get dressed up and go to a fancy party like that, but schmoozing isn't exactly my thing."

"And I'd rather skip the party all together." Ruby scrunched her nose. "So, how are things with you and Jake?"

"Really good, I think."

"You think?" Ruby asked.

"Well, it's all still really new, you know? I'm not sure where it's headed, but the sex is great, and I really enjoy being with him, so we'll just see what happens."

"Sounds like a good attitude," Ruby agreed with a nod.

"After everything he's been through, he could use some sex and fun, right?"

"Exactly. What about you?" Megan asked, giving her friend a shrewd look. "You haven't been on a date since we moved to Virginia."

Ruby made a face. "I hate dating. Can't I just skip that part and settle down with someone?"

Megan laughed into her wine. "Not unless you want to go on one of those 'Married at First Sight' shows."

"Absolutely not."

Megan looked across the table at her friend. Ruby had on a black-and-white patterned knit dress with a chunky red necklace, a perfect example of her off-beat style. She was quirky and pretty and funny, and it was ridiculous that she kept herself locked in her tower at the castle most of the time. "You should set up an online dating profile."

"I've thought about online dating," Ruby admitted. "I should be good at it since I get to hide behind my computer."

"Then do it," Megan said. "Let's make you a profile when we get home. I'll help."

"Well...maybe." Ruby looked away, sucking her bottom lip between her teeth. "I guess I've gotten comfortable being by myself."

"That's why online dating could be a good first step for you. Just see who's out there, see if anyone catches your interest. No harm in that, right?"

Ruby polished off her glass of wine. "True. Have you tried it?"

"Surprisingly enough, I haven't." Megan had always enjoyed going to parties and bars and never had trouble finding a man to bring home at the end of the night. What would dating be like for her in the future, though, after she and Jake had run their course? Would she set up an online dating profile? Would she reveal her scars in her profile photo? Would anyone click on it if she did?

"See, that's the difference between you and me," Ruby said thoughtfully. "You're just naturally good at this, and I'm not."

"I don't know about that. We'll find you a man...or a woman." Megan smiled as she remembered that night during their freshman year in college when Ruby had called to gush about the woman she'd kissed after her study group. As surprised as Megan had been to learn her friend was bisexual, part of her hadn't been surprised at all. "See, you've got an even wider dating pool to tap into than I do."

"All right," Ruby said with a definitive nod. "You've convinced me. Let's do it."

They finished up their meal and headed out. When they got back to the castle, Megan paused in the foyer, her eyes on the library. "Did you know Jake's an author?"

"Yes," Ruby said.

"Of course, you did," Megan said, giving her a good-natured nudge with her shoulder. "I think his books are in Theo's library."

"They are," Ruby told her, tucking a loose strand of hair behind her ear. "And yes, you should totally read them. Let me know if they're any good."

"I think I will. You get us some wine, and I'll meet you upstairs. I've got to feed and walk all the dogs first." Megan wandered into the library, running her hand over the weathered spines of the books nearest to her. She remembered Theo telling them that his grandfather had stocked the whole library himself. Each shelf had a little brass-plated marker, labeling what it contained. She found a shelf of classics, encyclopedias, English history, science fiction, historical fiction, mysteries, and in the far corner...local authors.

Front and center were five crisp, new books by Jake Tappen.

She felt herself smiling as she lifted one of them. She opened it, flipping to the "About the author" page at the back of the book, where a ridiculously handsome photo of Jake smiled back at her. He had on a button-down shirt, jeans, and leather boots, leaning against a fence with rolling green hills behind him.

Her throat went dry. Damn, she had it bad for this man. Tonight, she was going to take him to bed with her...figuratively, anyway, and she was absolutely not going to acknowledge that doing so wasn't really putting much space between them after all. She grinned as she tucked the book under her arm, headed for the stairs.

～

JAKE HAD WOKEN ALONE ALMOST every morning of his twenty-eight years. He'd never thought much about it, except during those first few months after Alana's accident when he'd still wished so fervently for her recovery so she could take her rightful place in his bed. Today, though, he woke filled with the memory of yesterday morning.

Megan in his bed. Her warm, soft body pressed against his. The way it had felt to hold and kiss her in these sleepy first moments of the day. Now that he knew what it was like to wake with a woman in his bed, the starkness of her absence left him cold.

He'd spent too many mornings alone. Too many days alone. Too many long, dark nights alone. He didn't want to be alone anymore, although he wasn't sure he was ready for the alternative yet, either. Because the thought of having Megan in his bed every morning, as much as it pleased him on a physical level, felt overwhelmingly new and strange. It was best that they were keeping things casual, taking it slow.

So, he got up and got ready for his day, went through his morning routine at the barn. He'd only been at Rosemont Castle for two weeks, but already this routine felt comfortable and familiar. He worked with Duchess, pleased with her progress. Mr. Nichols had mentioned a friend of his who had a horse that needed some training. Unlike Duchess, this horse was older, had been ridden for years but had some bad habits his owner would like corrected.

That was trickier than what Jake was doing with Duchess, but it was exactly the kind of challenge he looked forward to, not to mention the kind of business he needed. He couldn't afford to screw this up, which meant his work with Duchess was more crucial than ever.

As lunchtime approached, he moved Bug and Dusty from the pasture where they'd been enjoying some grass to the riding ring, now that he'd finished working with Duchess. They were able to graze for a few hours a day now without upsetting their systems.

Both horses had calmed considerably since arriving at the castle. In his experience, animals were intuitive that way. They easily saw who to trust and who wasn't worthy of it. He led one horse in each hand, turning his head to see Megan walking down the lane with two dogs at her side. She raised a hand to wave, and everything inside him seemed to warm at the sight of her.

Bug looked over at Megan and then shuffled to the side, knocking into Jake, the whites of her eyes gleaming as she tossed her head in alarm.

"Whoa, girl." He took a step back, keeping slack on her lead so she wouldn't feel trapped and panic further. What had startled her? "Easy now."

Bug danced sideways, her haunches slamming into Dusty, who yanked the line in Jake's right hand. He moved with them, keeping his voice low and soothing while he tried to figure out what was spooking Bug. He hadn't heard or seen anything likely to startle her. The only other person anywhere in sight was Megan.

Megan *and* her foster dogs. Bug's wounds had been caused when she was attacked by feral dogs.

"Megan, can you take those dogs into the farmhouse for a few minutes?" he said calmly.

She nodded, her eyes wide, posture tense. But thank goodness she'd had the sense not to express her own fear in a way that might have further frightened Bug. She led the dogs toward the farmhouse, taking them in through the front door. Almost immediately, Bug began to relax. She pranced uneasily, snorting as she looked around for any further sign of a threat.

"Easy, girl. The dogs are gone." He kept talking to her until she'd calmed before leading her and Dusty the rest of the way to the arena. Once they were happily munching hay in the sunshine, he headed to the farmhouse. He found Megan in the living room, still holding her dogs on leash, her expression a mixture of guilt and worry.

"Everything okay?" she asked when she saw him.

"Fine."

"I'm so sorry. I should have asked before I brought the dogs down to the barn."

"I would have told you to bring them," he said as he closed the distance between them, pulling her in for a gentle kiss. "Dogs and farms go hand-in-hand. Bug may have some issues from that dog attack before she got here."

"I never even thought of that. I just thought the dogs might like to meet the horses." She stiffened in his arms. "Poor Bug."

"It's all right. We'll work her through it. And Twister loves dogs if you want to introduce them." He glanced at the dogs sniffing around their feet. One had shaggy black fur, while the other was a light tan color, like a lab.

"Okay," she murmured against his lips. "In a minute, maybe."

"Missed you this morning." He sank his hands into the back pockets of her jeans, securing her closer against him, breathing in her scent as he kissed her.

"Yeah?"

"Yeah." He pinched her ass. "How do you feel about staying here tonight?"

"That depends," she said, giving him a coy look. "How do you feel about dogs?"

He looked at the two standing beside them. "I like dogs."

"Well, that's good, because I hate to impose, but these two are my responsibility until they're adopted. I can have Elle watch them for me sometimes, but if you want me to sleep over often, it would make things a lot easier if I could bring them with me."

"Fine with me if it's okay with you guys," Jake said to the dogs. The shaggy black one gave an excited bark in response. "I've never had a dog, but I've been around plenty of them in the barns where I've worked."

"These guys are pretty easygoing," she said. "Barnaby—the light-colored one—is really shy. You'll barely know he's here. Chandler is pretty enthusiastic, but he doesn't really get into any trouble. As long as we close them in the bedroom with us so they don't wander, they should be fine."

"Okay, then."

"Do you think I should go check on Bug?" she asked, her brow wrinkling.

"Nah, she's fine. The dogs just startled her."

She gripped his T-shirt and pulled him in for another kiss. "I'll see you tonight, then?"

"Yep." He watched as she gathered her dogs and headed out the front door, wondering yet again why the house felt so empty every time she walked out that door.

~

ON HER WAY back to the castle from Jake's house, Megan bumped into Elle out walking her own foster dogs. "Hey! How was your charity thing last night with Theo?"

"It was great," Elle said brightly. "I think I'm getting the hang of this future-wife-of-an-earl thing."

"You never didn't have the hang of it," Megan told her. "But I'm glad you're feeling more confident about it now."

"I heard I missed quite an exciting night for you." Elle raised her eyebrows. "Or the recap of it, anyway. So, things are going well for you and Jake?"

"Yeah." She felt herself smiling. "I still feel kind of irresponsible for sleeping with him while he's our tenant, but, well... here we are."

Elle laughed. "You know who that sounds like, right?"

"You, last year with Theo." Megan shook her head. "But just because it worked out for you guys doesn't make it a good idea for me and Jake."

"Doesn't make it a bad one either," Elle said with a meaningful look. "I'm just glad things are good, and hopefully we can all get together for a girls' night soon."

"Definitely," Megan said. "If we don't hurry up, our next girls' night will be your bachelorette party."

"Yeah, oh my God." Elle rubbed at her forehead. "It's all coming up so soon."

Megan rested a hand on Elle's arm. "Are you feeling better about the wedding? I mean, about getting married at the Langdon family estate?"

She blew out a breath. "Yeah. It'll be nerve-wracking, no way around it, but you guys made me feel a lot better about things. And expect me to lean on you pretty heavily while we're there."

"Totally what we're here for." Megan leaned in to give her a quick hug, which was interrupted by leashes tugging them in various directions as their dogs started tackling each other, rolling around in the grass.

After chatting with Elle for a few more minutes, Megan brought Barnaby and Chandler inside. She spent a few minutes doing obedience exercises with them before settling them in her room. It was her afternoon to run the inn.

She brought Jake's book—the one she'd taken from the library yesterday—downstairs with her to read in her downtime. She'd started it last night after she left Ruby's room, and then she'd accidentally stayed up way too late reading. It was good. Really good. She didn't often make time to read, but right now she was dying to know what happened next for Derrick the PI as he tried to track down a missing horse trainer. The missing woman's boyfriend had been found dead right before Megan finally gave in to her drooping eyelids last night.

Downstairs, she tabbed through the reservation software on the tablet in their office to familiarize herself with today's schedule. They had three couples scheduled to check in. She ran through their daily routine, answering emails and updating their social media. Today, she uploaded some photos she'd taken of the new blooms in the garden, inviting people to come and experience spring at Rosemont Castle.

Once that was taken care of, she wandered into the library and settled with her book to wait for their guests to arrive. Derrick the PI had just been overtaken by an intruder when the guest doorbell rang. Megan reluctantly put down the book and went to greet their new arrivals. A couple in their fifties stood just inside the castle's front doors, looking around with awestruck looks on their faces.

"Hi," Megan said as she approached. "Checking in?"

"Yes," the woman replied, tearing her gaze from the elaborate chandelier overhead. "We're the Westmores."

Megan consulted the tablet in her arms. "Mary and Art Westmore. Staying for two nights?"

"That's right," Mary confirmed. Her eyes locked briefly on the left side of Megan's face before sliding away.

"Great," Megan said, trying to ignore the heat that crept across her skin, the way her scar seemed to ache in moments like these, when she became so hyperaware of it.

Mary Westmore kept her gaze firmly anywhere but Megan's face as they completed the check-in process and Megan walked them upstairs to their room. After she'd gotten them settled, she stood for a moment in the hallway, her back against the wall, one hand pressed against her diaphragm, as she breathed past the tears burning her throat and stinging her eyes.

She shouldn't let it bother her. It was Mary Westmore's problem, not Megan's. She knew this, but it didn't do anything to quiet the storm raging inside her. She would have to deal with other people's discomfort with her scars for the rest of her life. So, when would it stop bothering her? How long until she got over her own discomfort with her face? What if that day never came?

~

Jake finished up at the barn early that night, so he'd have plenty of time to get ready for his date with Megan. He'd texted her earlier, suggesting they get dinner in town. It had been so damn long since he'd taken a woman out to dinner. He hadn't done it since he was old enough to truly enjoy it, and he couldn't wait to treat Megan to a nice evening out.

He topped off the water troughs in all the pastures and walked to the barn to get Bug and Dusty, who'd been in their stalls since he worked with them earlier, drawing up short when he spied the door to Bug's stall standing ajar. It had been latched securely when he left. He was sure of it. Tamping back his alarm, he walked briskly to Bug's stall, alarm morphing into relief as he saw Megan inside, talking quietly to the little horse as she rubbed her neck.

She glanced over at him as he stepped inside the stall. She stood with her lower back against the wall, legs spread for balance as she spoke softly to Bug, who was nosing at her with more interest and affection than Jake had seen yet from the horse. "You ladies having a pow wow in here or what?"

"Yep," Megan answered, her lips curving slightly. Her hair was in her face, an outward manifestation of whatever internal battle she was waging against herself.

"She's doing really well." He gestured to Bug, who gave him a curious glance. She'd filled in considerably since she arrived, and her wounds were healing nicely too.

"She reminds me of a unicorn or something with her purple patches," Megan said.

"You hiding your magical powers from us, Bug?" he asked. She nuzzled his hand, searching for treats. "Sorry, girl. You caught me empty-handed."

"She looks like she could be," Megan said. "Hiding magical powers, that is. You know how superheroes and their animal sidekicks have their incognito personas when they're not fighting the bad guys? Bug looks like that to me, like she could transform into a magical creature that carries a superhero into battle."

"Who's the superhero in that scenario?" Jake asked.

"You?" she suggested with a soft smile, darting a glance over at him. Her hair still covered her scars, and he wondered if this was her incognito persona too. He wished she could see herself the way he saw her, strong and brave and beautiful.

"Nah, definitely you," he told her. "I'm getting Wonder Woman vibes."

"Hardly," she scoffed, keeping her gaze solidly on Bug. "This one, though…"

Bug's coat was unique, mostly white with dappled spots that suggested some Appaloosa heritage, and those purple splotches around her face and neck. Her mane was short and spikey, like a mohawk, adding to her somewhat comical appearance.

"Now I'll forever see her as an undercover superhero," he said, stepping closer to slide an arm around Megan's shoulders.

She leaned against him. "Do you think she'll find a home soon? That either of them will?"

"I don't know," he answered honestly. "I've never worked with rescue horses before. I have no idea what the average adoption timeframe is, and these guys aren't even officially on the market yet, right?"

She shook her head, her silky brown hair falling over his arm. "They will be soon, though."

"Are you ready for dinner?" he asked. It was an hour before they'd arranged to meet, and she was wearing the same clothes she'd had on when he saw her earlier—not that there was anything wrong with the way she looked, but he knew women usually liked to change before they went out. He hadn't expected to see her here in the barn, and as glad as he was for it, he also felt like she might have come here for an escape... from what, he wasn't sure.

"No," she answered, confirming his suspicion. "I just stopped in to see Bug."

"I'm finishing up early so I can get myself cleaned up in time." He gestured to his clothes, bearing the dust and dirt of a day on the farm.

"I won't keep you, then," she said. "I've got to get ready too. I'll meet you at the farmhouse at seven?"

He nodded. "You're bringing the dogs with you, right?"

"Actually, I thought I should bring them down after we get back from dinner, so I don't have to leave them unattended in your house before I've had a chance to get them settled."

"Okay." He watched as she closed and latched the door to Bug's stall before drawing her into his arms. He held on to her for a long minute, hoping she was okay, wishing he could undo whatever had upset her. "So, I'll see you in an hour."

## 12

*J*ake gazed across the table at Megan. She had on a simple black dress that was absolutely stunning on her. There was something mesmerizing about her, an energy that seemed to radiate from her. He couldn't look away, not that he was trying to. Tonight, she wore her hair pulled into a loose knot at her neck, draped low over the left side of her face to partially conceal her scars.

She looked up, and their eyes locked. "This is really nice."

"I think so too." He'd brought her to a steakhouse in town he'd been wanting to visit. "I've always heard great things about this place."

"You've never eaten here before?" she asked before taking another bite of her salad.

"Couldn't afford it back in high school when I was dating Alana, and never had anyone to bring after that. There are a bunch of restaurants here in town I'd love to try now that I have an excuse to eat there." He smiled to keep the mood light, not wanting her to feel sad on his behalf. He'd felt plenty of sadness and awkwardness over his situation in the past, but tonight there was nothing but joy and relief to be out to dinner with a beautiful woman who would be spending tonight in his bed. Finally, he could enjoy these simple, *normal* things like everyone else.

"Well, as it happens, I love any excuse to go out and enjoy a good meal, so it sounds like this might be a mutually beneficial situation." She winked, brushing at the hair that covered her cheek. Both of them were keeping their scars hidden tonight, but maybe that was okay. Maybe they deserved to enjoy themselves for a night without having to think about the darker parts of their lives.

"I did a little research this afternoon," he told her. "And I have a plan to help Bug with her fear of dogs."

"Oh yeah?" Megan's eyes brightened.

"Yeah. It would make her a lot more appealing to potential adopters if we could get her past that. Dogs are common on farms, so it could be a problem for her."

"I didn't even think of that, but yeah, you're right. She already has so many strikes against her, it would be great if we could get rid of at least one of them."

"I wouldn't say that. She's very young, which works in her favor. Once she's trained, she could make a wonderful horse for the right person."

"She'll be scarred," Megan said, her gaze dropping to her salad plate. "Statistically, animals with physical imperfections are more difficult to adopt."

"I'm not familiar with the statistics, but she's a pretty horse." *And you're a beautiful woman.* "I think she's going to look great once she's not purple anymore."

Megan smiled softly. "I don't know. I kind of like her unicorn spots."

"It does give her that superhero vibe," he agreed. "I've been busy with my offsite clients and Duchess, but she's progressing really nicely in her training. Once I have some free time, I'll try to work with Bug and Dusty, see if I can start some saddle work. Assuming of course that neither of them have had any training yet. They may surprise us."

"I feel bad that you're spending so much time on them, but I really appreciate it."

"Don't feel bad. It's not like you're asking me to train a horse for free. I'm helping out with a local rescue. There's a difference, and I like to be involved."

"I enjoy it too," she said. "Working with the shelter on the Fairy Tails program has been one of the most rewarding things since I started working at Rosemont Castle."

"It's not something I had much experience with in the past. I'm glad I do now."

The waitress arrived with their entrees, and conversation slowed as they ate. After a long day at the barn, he had worked up quite an appetite, and his steak turned out to be every bit as delicious as he'd hoped.

"This is so good," Megan said around a bite. She'd gotten beef medallions in a brown sauce that smelled delicious.

"Jake?"

He turned to find himself facing Sylvia Gayle and her husband, Bob. The couple were close friends of the Robertsons, and Jake had spent plenty of time with them over the years. Nice enough people, if a bit set in their ways.

"Mrs. Gayle, it's good to see you." Jake made introductions, noticing Sylvia's obvious interest in Megan. He wasn't exactly trying to keep their relationship under wraps, but now that Sylvia knew, his in-laws would probably hear about it before the end of the night. If he'd taken the time to think about it, he would have preferred to tell them himself, but there was no changing it now.

"You're one of the women working up at Rosemont Castle, aren't you?" Sylvia asked Megan, who nodded.

"That's right. We've been managing the property for almost a year now."

"I've heard wonderful things about it," Sylvia said. "I know a lot of people who've been out for the tours you're giving."

"That's great," Megan told her with a warm smile. "We're all really enjoying it."

They chatted for a few more minutes while Sylvia plainly sized up Megan to report back to the Robertsons, and he tried not to let it bother him.

"What's the matter?" Megan asked once the Gayles had left.

"Sylvia is probably already on the phone with Tina...Alana's mother." He shrugged, but it felt stiff, even to him. "I hadn't thought about how people would react."

"I'm sorry," she murmured.

"Don't be. It just caught me off guard, that's all. It's the only downside of small-town living." He shrugged. "Everyone's in your business all the time."

"Isn't that the truth," Megan said.

"Story of my life. The whole town's been fascinated with me since Alana's accident. People always get nosy about that kind of thing, but then there were the rumors about my, you know, virginity." He lowered his voice to a near-whisper on that last word. "I guess I should have expected it to be a big deal for people to see me out with someone new."

"Well, if we eat our way around downtown like we were planning, hopefully it will lose its novelty," Megan suggested.

He nodded. "You're right. The more we let them see us, the quicker they'll get over it and hopefully quit paying attention to me at all. I won't have to be that tragic guy everyone feels sorry for anymore."

She pressed a hand over his against the cream-colored tablecloth. "Then I think we should make it our mission to erase Tragic Jake from their narrative as quickly as possible."

"Yes." He met her eyes. "Please."

They made it through the rest of their meal without interruption, and he drove them back to the castle, pulling in at the farmhouse. He shut off the engine, his right hand finding hers in the semi-darkness of the truck cab. "I had a really great time tonight."

"Me too." Her voice was hushed, her fingers wrapped tightly around his.

And he couldn't wait another moment to kiss her. He leaned in, brushing his lips against hers. It was dizzying how much his life had changed in the last few weeks if he really took the time to acknowledge it. Overwhelming, maybe, but not necessarily in a bad way. Not when it all felt this good.

And then Megan's hand was in his lap, her palm pressed against his cock, and he was certain that it was all good. So good. They fumbled around in the front seat of the truck, touching and kissing, arms and legs bumping into various surfaces as they struggled for contact. Megan's elbow bumped the switch for the interior light, causing them both to squint against the sudden glare, laughing.

"What do you say we take this inside?" he suggested.

"Excellent idea." She straightened the bodice of her dress and reached for her purse.

"Do you need to go get your dogs first?" he asked as he climbed out of the truck. As much as he really didn't mind having her dogs around tonight, the thought of letting her go right now, even for a few minutes, felt like absolute torture.

Either she saw it in his eyes, or she was feeling the same way, because she gave her head a small shake before draping herself against his body. "Let's enjoy ourselves first. Once I get them, I'll have to spend time getting them settled, and I don't think I can wait that long to get you naked."

"I couldn't agree more." His hips were already moving against hers as he stepped her backward toward the farmhouse. He might not ever get used to the feeling of having her in his arms, the pleasure of her touch, the fire it caused inside him, a burning need that only seemed to grow stronger each time he held her.

He'd barely closed the door behind them before Megan had him pressed against it, her hands untucking his shirt from his jeans, skimming over his bare skin, causing his brain to incinerate with lust and need.

One of her hands drifted down to palm him. "You're so hard," she murmured.

"Always," he whispered into her mouth. "Always with you."

She squeezed him through his jeans, and he locked his knees to keep them upright. He spun them so her back was against the door, his hand beneath her dress, stroking her through her panties. Then her legs were wrapped around his waist, his cock pressed between her legs, their hips moving frantically as their tongues tangled, hands grasping at fabric.

"Right here," she gasped. "Now."

"Hell, yes." He shoved a hand into his back pocket, supporting Megan with the other, trying to summon enough brainpower to find the condom he'd put in his wallet. He grabbed it, letting the wallet fall to the floor, as Megan unbuttoned his jeans and eased the zipper down, freeing his cock. She took the foil packet from his fingers and covered him, pushing her panties to the side as she guided him to her entrance.

He groaned as he sank inside her. "So good."

"Mm." Her eyes slid shut as her body gripped him, and then he was moving, thrusting into her with one arm braced against the door, the other around her waist to hold her steady, although her legs were wrapped so tightly around his hips, he doubted she would have budged even without him holding her.

"Fuck, yes." He pounded into her, and damn, he hoped she was getting close, because something about taking her against the door was really doing it for him. "Oh, damn, baby, you feel so good."

In response, her heels dug into the backs of his thighs, reminding him she still had on her heels, which only turned him on more. The hallway filled with the sounds of sex, heavy breathing, the slap of skin against skin, and their occasional moans and cries of pleasure. Everything about it only drove him closer to the edge.

Megan's head fell back against the wood behind her, eyes shut, mouth slightly open. Her hands clenched around his ass, and then he felt her orgasm pulsing through her, gripping him, hard. That was all he needed to join her, shouting his release as he emptied himself inside her.

He managed to walk them backward to the couch before his legs gave out, dropping them in a heap onto the leather upholstery. "That does it," he muttered, resting his head against the cushion behind him as he caught his breath. "We're going to have to christen every room—and maybe every wall—in the house."

Megan gave a throaty laugh, rolling over to sit beside him. She tugged at her dress, sliding it back into place. "I'd be happy to help you out with that."

He wrapped an arm around her shoulders, drawing her in against him. As much as he wanted to sit there with her forever, he needed to get rid of the condom. He removed it, tucked himself back inside his jeans, and stood. "Don't go anywhere," he called as he walked into the bathroom.

"Actually, this is probably a good time to go get the dogs. If I stay here any longer, we're going to get too comfortable—and naked—for me to want to go back out."

"True enough. Want a hand?"

"Yeah, actually. Sure."

So, they cleaned up together in the bathroom and walked up the drive to the castle. He followed her upstairs to her bedroom, taking it in with open curiosity as she gathered the dogs from their crates. He'd been in the public spaces of the castle several times now but had never been into any of the guest rooms, let alone Megan's bedroom. It was as girly as he would have expected, with a bedspread in shades of purple and white lacey curtains.

A Jake Tappen novel lay in the middle of the bed.

~

MEGAN TURNED to find Jake holding the book in his right hand, brow raised expectantly.

"A little light reading?" he asked.

She shrugged, not even trying to hide her smile. "I told you I was going to read your books."

"I thought you were just humoring me."

"Nope. I was totally serious, and I'm really enjoying it too." She slid the book from his hand, setting it on her nightstand. "In fact, I think I'm going to buy a copy so you can sign it for me."

"Where did you get that one?" He sat on the edge of her bed, greeting Chandler, who had bounded over and shoved his head in Jake's lap.

"From the library downstairs."

"I've read several books from Theo's library myself these last few weeks," Jake admitted.

"Oh yeah? What kind of books do you like to read?" she asked as she threw a change of clothes and toiletries into an overnight bag, along with a few treats and things for the dogs.

"Mysteries mostly, crime thrillers. I like it when an author totally blows my mind with a plot twist at the end of the book."

"I should have guessed, based on what you write." She picked up her bag and leashed the dogs. "So, are you going to blow my mind with a plot twist at the end?"

"You'll have to let me know." He took Barnaby's leash from her, and they walked downstairs together.

Theo passed them in the hallway, headed toward the kitchen. "Hi, Megan," he said absently before his eyebrows raised in an almost comical expression as he took in the entirety of the scene in front of him. "Jake."

"Hi, Theo," Jake answered, his expression betraying nothing.

"Have a good evening, you two," Theo called over his shoulder with a grin as he walked away.

Megan laughed under her breath as they made their way out the front door. Between the overnight bag and the dogs, it couldn't have been any more obvious that she was on her way to spend the night at the farmhouse. "Well, if Elle hadn't already told him, he knows now."

"I don't think Elle had told him, judging by the look on his face."

"It doesn't matter," she told him. "There aren't any rules saying we can't do what we're doing, and after he hooked up with Elle last year while she was working here at the castle, he's the last person to judge."

"He would never judge," Jake said, a frown tugging at his lips. "But it's still not exactly the impression I wanted to make as his new tenant."

"Hey." She rested her free hand on his arm. "It's okay, really. Theo doesn't care. He likes us both. He's probably just happy to see you dating again."

"You're right." Jake shook his head slightly as if to clear it. "This is all so new to me. I haven't dated since high school. Everything feels awkward."

"I'm sure it does, but you'll get used to it."

They walked outside, taking the trail that led past the horse pastures so Chandler and Barnaby could sniff around and take care of any business before they got to the farmhouse. It was a beautiful evening, crisp and cool with all the fresh scents of spring hanging in the air, flowers and grass and damp earth.

Back at the farmhouse, she unclipped the leashes from both dogs and set down a bowl of water for them in the kitchen. Chandler sniffed around energetically, while Barnaby stayed close to Megan, trailing her around the living room. Jake pulled her in for a kiss, and Chandler—sensing a fun new game in the works—ran over and jumped up, putting his front paws on Jake's thigh to join in.

"Not used to having a dog underfoot," Jake said, grinning.

"Down, Chandler," she told the dog firmly, and he hopped

down, barking as if he didn't approve of being left out of the hugging and kissing.

That was pretty much the theme of their evening. She and Jake made it to bed, only to have Barnaby and Chandler trample across them several times while they were having sex, which led to a lot of laughter and mumbled threats to throw them out of the room.

"They'll settle down," Megan said as she lay against Jake's chest afterward. "They've never been here before, and they aren't quite sure what they're supposed to be doing."

"Either that, or it's their mission to make sure I never get a dog," he said, but there was no heat behind his words. On the contrary, he'd seemed more amused than annoyed by the dogs' antics.

"You should adopt one." She rubbed her fingers absently through his chest hair, enjoying the way it tickled her skin.

"One of these?" He looked over at Barnaby and Chandler, who had finally settled on the spare blanket they'd spread on the floor as a makeshift dog bed.

"No, not those guys necessarily, but a farmhouse should have a dog, don't you think?"

"Yeah, I like the idea of that." He sounded relaxed and content. "I think I've lived alone enough for this lifetime, don't you?"

## 13

*J*ake woke up feeling unusually warm all over. He opened his eyes to find Barnaby the dog curled up against his chest, tail alarmingly close to Jake's face. He rolled to his back, registering another heavy form settled over his feet at about the same time he saw Megan sprawled across the bed on his other side.

A smile tugged at his lips. Now *there* was a welcome sight first thing in the morning. He rolled to face her, running a hand through the chestnut strands of hair fanning across her pillow. His heart felt so full, it was almost uncomfortable. Mostly, he couldn't be happier to have Megan in his bed. A big part of him felt like he'd found what he'd been missing for so long.

But a smaller part of him felt trapped beneath the weight of two dogs and one sleeping woman. He'd lived alone for so long, maybe that's all he was suited for anymore. But no, that couldn't be true. After all, how many nights had he lain awake, feeling so alone, so empty he thought he might implode from the crushing weight of it? This was just an adjustment period. And so, with a dog against his back, a dog on his feet, and a beautiful woman in front of him, he closed his eyes, willing himself to relax.

The next thing he was aware of was Megan's soft laughter. Groggily, he blinked at her, realizing he must have fallen back to sleep.

"Sorry about them," she whispered, pressing her lips against his. "They usually stay in their crates at night."

"I guess they wanted to join the sleepover party," he said, drawing her closer against him.

"Can't really blame them," she murmured as her naked body landed flush against his, discovering his morning wood.

"All the same, I don't think I want them around for this part, do you?" He pressed his cock into the heat between her legs. It was only the second time in his whole life that he'd awakened with a woman in his bed, and he was still somewhat overwhelmed by the freedom to lose himself in her welcome body in these gentle morning moments instead of laying here alone as he'd done so many damn times, deciding whether to ignore his cock or attempt to relieve his loneliness with his own fist.

"Off the bed," Megan announced, shooing the dogs toward their blanket by the door.

Chandler let out a bark of protest but did as he was told. Barnaby hopped down quietly. Once the bed was dog-free, Jake retrieved a condom. As he pushed inside her, he forgot everything but the overwhelming pleasure they shared. Sex was somehow softer and gentler in these moments, while their bodies were still sluggish from sleep, but the rush of pleasure he felt as he came inside her far surpassed the energizing power of coffee.

They showered together and shared bagels and coffee in the kitchen before Megan began gathering her things. "I need to get these guys back to the castle. I've got a portrait session booked at nine."

"And I need to get down to the barn." He drew her in for one last kiss. "Will I see you later?"

"Sure." Her smile seemed charged with the energy of the sun. "Text me."

"Will do. Good luck with your portrait session."

"It's a family who adopted a dog from us last month. I can't wait to see them again." She clipped leashes onto the dogs, slung her duffel bag over her shoulders, and headed for the door. "I'll talk to you later."

"Later." He stood there in the kitchen for several minutes, absorbing the stillness and quiet in her wake. No dogs barking or sniffing around his kitchen. No laughter or happy chatter over breakfast. His ears rang with the silence.

Unsure what to make of it, he headed down to the barn. After he'd finished Duchess's training session, he spent some time with Dusty Star, discovering that she accepted a bridle and saddle readily. He took her for a walk around the property, thrilled to know she could be ridden.

By the time he made it back to the farmhouse, it was past one, and he was starved. He fixed himself a sandwich and guzzled a can of soda. His phone buzzed with an incoming text as he was cleaning up his lunch, and a thrill resonated inside him that it could be Megan. He couldn't wait to see her again.

*Beers tonight at Bar None?* It was from his buddy Sean.

A different kind of thrill buzzed through his system, because his friends would probably want to hear about his new relationship with Megan, and he wasn't sure he was ready to talk about it yet.

*Tucker and Theo are already in*, Sean texted.

*Okay*, Jake agreed, knowing it was probably easier to just get this over with. Maybe it wouldn't be that bad. Maybe he could use their advice. Maybe.

Restless, he wandered toward the castle under the guise of returning a book he'd borrowed from Theo's library, halfway hoping he might bump into Megan. He wanted to tell her about Dusty's progress, and hell, he just wanted to see her. Instead, he found Theo.

"Any good?" Theo asked, gesturing to the book Jake was putting back on the shelf.

"Not bad, but I figured out whodunit about halfway through."

"Well, that's no good," Theo said, his lips quirking in a smile.

"To be fair, I have a habit of doing that."

"Probably what makes you so good at writing them," Theo commented, reaching to pick up a different book.

"Could be," Jake agreed.

"I hear we're meeting Tucker and Sean later?" Theo said, turning the book over absently to read the back cover.

"Yeah."

Theo put the book back on the shelf and turned to leave. "I'm going to have James drive me. You're welcome to ride along, just meet me up here around seven."

"I think I'll take you up on that. Thanks." He wouldn't mind not having to drive tonight or the chance to get to know Theo better.

"Absolutely. No sense taking two cars to the same place." Theo left the library, headed toward his office in the rear of the castle while Jake headed for the front door.

As he walked down the path toward the farmhouse, he was still plagued by the uneasy, restless feeling he'd had since he woke that morning. Without fully realizing where he was headed, he climbed in his truck and started driving. The castle's winding drive gave way to a series of mountain roads that he knew by heart. He bypassed downtown, instead driving toward the Towering Pines Baptist Church.

In the back of his mind, he'd realized this was his destination, but it wasn't until he was walking through the cemetery toward Alana's grave that he realized how much he needed to be here. He knelt in front of her headstone, wishing he'd had the foresight to bring flowers or something to leave here for her.

A fresh arrangement of pink roses—Alana's favorite—

already sat in front of the headstone, no doubt left by her parents, who still visited her at least once a week. Jake hadn't been here in over a month, not since he moved into Rosemont Castle. He pressed his fingers against the cold stone, feeling an ache in his heart that might never heal.

"Been thinking of you a lot," he said quietly. "Wondering what you'd think about the direction my life has taken this year, wishing you were here with me for it." But as he spoke the words, he realized the sentiment behind them felt almost abstract. Alana had only been buried for a year, but she'd been gone for a decade. What would she have been doing with her own life in her late twenties? Would they have already started a family together?

"You'd like Megan." This he was sure of. Alana hadn't exactly been hard to get along with. She was one of those effortlessly outgoing people who liked virtually everyone she met. She and Megan had the same way of looking through the bullshit in life to see the beauty most people missed.

With Alana, it had come through her faith. She would meet a total stranger, share a conversation more meaningful than anything he'd managed in a month, and pray for them the next day in church. Megan used the lens of her camera to explore the beauty of the world around her. He knew she was hiding behind it a little bit this year, since her accident, but from what she'd told him, photography had always been her passion.

She'd shown him some of the photos she'd taken of him with the horses, and he was blown away by what she'd captured. Not just the mechanics of his training sessions with Duchess, but the animal's spirit, the light in her eyes, the fluidity of her movement. It was impressive. She had real talent.

As he stood there in the cemetery, facing Alana's grave, the restlessness inside him stilled. Maybe this was peace. Maybe Alana had granted it to him, or maybe he'd found it on his own. Either way, coming here had been the right decision.

"I'll be back soon," he promised before he walked back to his truck and drove away.

~

*I HAVE SOME GOOD NEWS.*

Megan stared at the text from Jake, a spark pinging through her belly at the sight of his name. *Oh yeah?*

*I rode Dusty this morning. She's solid under the saddle.*

That was so far from whatever she'd expected his news to be that she sucked in an audible breath, sitting up straighter on her bed. *Wow. Really? That \*is\* good news!*

*Yeah, I'll spend some time working with her, but I think it's safe to list her as rideable when she goes up for adoption.*

*That's wonderful,* she replied.

*It is. I'm having dinner with the Robertsons and then going out with the guys tonight. Want to do something tomorrow?*

*Definitely. Enjoy your night.*

She set her phone down, disappointment mixing with relief that she wouldn't see him tonight. When they were together, everything felt so intense and wonderful and *right* that she never wanted it to end. But right now, when she had the clarity of a little distance from him, she knew it was all too much too soon.

Space was good. Because neither of them needed anything serious right now.

She flopped on her bed and almost immediately felt paws slam into her chest, knocking the air from her lungs. "Oof." She reached out a hand, combing it through Chandler's shaggy dark fur. He lay with his front half across her, brown eyes bright as he tried to decide whether to snuggle or wrestle.

"You're too big for this, dude," she mumbled, pushing him to the mattress beside her. Barnaby, not wanting to be left out, hopped up on the bed, tail wagging enthusiastically.

"Who are you talking to?" Ruby asked from the doorway.

"This creature," Megan said, tousling Chandler's shaggy head.

"Hey, ladies." Elle popped up next to Ruby in the doorway.

"What are you doing up here?" Ruby asked with an amused smile. It was true, though; Elle rarely visited this hallway anymore now that she'd moved into the owners' quarters.

"Looking for you, actually," Elle said. "The guys are going into town for beers tonight, so I thought we should have a girls' night."

"Jake told me the same thing," Megan said. "And I'm totally down for girls' night."

"But not at Bar None," Elle said. "Because that's where they're going. Remember that time we accidentally crashed their night when Theo and I were fighting?"

"The night I met Jake," Megan murmured, still flat on her back in bed with two dogs jockeying for position on top of her.

"Let's go to that new wine bar," Ruby suggested. "You can order delivery from any of the restaurants downtown."

"Sounds perfect to me," Elle said.

And so, three hours later, they were cozied up to a table in the rear of the bar with a platter of sushi in front of them and two open bottles of wine—because Ruby preferred white wine with sushi, while Elle and Megan were most of the way through their bottle of red.

"I have my first dress fitting on Friday," Elle said. "I'm so excited to see it, you know, not the sample dress, but the actual dress I'll be walking down the aisle in."

"Ooh, can we come?" Ruby asked.

"I was kind of hoping you would," Elle said, something a little sad in her smile. She'd lost her mom when she was ten, so she often leaned on her friends at times like these when she needed someone to fill these mother-daughter moments.

"I'll bring my camera," Megan said. "Get some shots of you seeing your dress for the first time." The sample dress Elle had tried on was ivory, but she'd ordered it with pink rhinestone embellishments around the bodice, and Megan could hardly wait to see it on her.

"I'm so lucky to have you guys." Elle's eyes went glossy.

"Likewise." They leaned in for a group hug, careful not to spill any of their wine.

"We're all lucky to have each other," Ruby said as they broke apart, and if Megan wasn't mistaken, her eyes were a bit glossy as well.

"Any action on your new online dating profile?" Megan asked as she picked up her chopsticks and went for some sushi.

Ruby scrunched her nose. "I've had a few messages, but nobody worth meeting. I'll keep looking, though."

"Definitely do," Elle told her. "Who knows, the future love of your life might contact you tomorrow."

"I don't know about that," Ruby said, taking a sip of her wine. "But I'll keep trying. Maybe soon we'll all have someone special in our lives."

Megan's thoughts drifted to Jake, imagining a future where they hung out with Elle and Theo, and Ruby and her date, before shaking it from her mind. Everything about her relationship with Jake was supposed to be simple and uncomplicated, but right now, it felt like the opposite.

# 14

---

*O*ver the next three weeks, Jake's new routines continued to solidify. He and Megan spent more and more time together. She often spent the night at the farmhouse with her foster dogs. He'd almost finished training Duchess. In fact, Mr. Nichols was coming out on Monday to see Jake's progress with her.

His training business was still off to a slow start, but he was trying not to worry too much about it. He'd picked up a new part-time client whom he visited twice a week for training sessions. In his spare time, he worked with Dusty. She had shaped up nicely as a trail horse and might even be suited for some light lesson work.

Bug's bite wounds healed, and she no longer had her magical purple spots. She was still too skittish to begin even basic saddle work, though. He'd concentrated his work with her so far on taking long walks around the property on a lead line to build her trust.

He'd just returned from one of these walks when he saw Megan standing by the upper pasture with Barnaby at her side, rubbing Twister as he hung his head over the fence.

Bug danced nervously at Jake's side, but she didn't panic at the sight of the dog. He and Megan had worked with her on this a lot over the past weeks, helping Bug to overcome her fear.

"Where's Chandler?" Jake asked, because he didn't often see her with one dog but not the other.

"He was adopted this morning," she told him with a smile.

"That's good news."

"It is. He seemed really happy with his new family. I think it was a good fit." Megan and Barnaby walked to the middle of the path in front of him and stopped.

Jake allowed Bug to approach at her own pace, head down and nostrils flaring as she sized up the dog at Megan's side. Barnaby was just the dog for the job too, always quiet and submissive. He stayed close to Megan as Bug approached.

"We've made a lot of progress with her, don't you think?" Megan said softly, watching as Bug sniffed at Barnaby from a few feet away. The dog watched, ears pricked, posture relaxed.

"We have," Jake agreed. "Most animals are pretty willing to work through their issues, if you just give them the chance."

"With the right person," she added.

"That's true."

"Look at that," Megan breathed as Bug put her nose right up to Barnaby. The dog stood, tail wagging, and greeted her, nose to nose. Megan pressed a hand over her mouth.

"See? She just needed a little patience." Jake stroked Bug's neck as she continued to sniff at the dog. "I'm going to go ahead and put her out with Dusty now, to make sure we end things on a good note."

Megan nodded, following him toward the pasture. "The Spring Fling festival is this weekend. Will you be there?"

He nodded. "Most of the town will be. Have you been before?"

"No. We had just moved here last year this time and missed all the hype. But this year, we're going to have a table during the vendor fair to advertise our program here at the castle, right next to the shelter's table so we can show off our foster dogs."

"Minus one," he commented as he put Bug in the pasture, securing the gate behind her. He led the way into the barn.

"Yeah. I'll get a new foster, but probably not before the festival. I think Priya's already picked out a little poodle mix for me."

"A poodle mix, huh? Sounds kind of frou-frou," Jake said with a smile, looking down at Barnaby, who was currently rolling around on the barn's dirt floor, paws waving in the air.

"Sometimes the frou-frou dogs are the easiest to adopt." She looked down at Barnaby and shook her head with a smile. "This guy loves the barn."

"He'd be a good barn dog." Jake knelt, and Barnaby rolled to his feet, bounding toward him. Chandler, while more outgoing and sociable, had been too unpredictable to have around the horses, darting underneath them and barking in a way that had made both of the rescue horses nervous. Quiet, steady Barnaby had been the obvious choice for their work with Bug.

"He's so shy that he's had trouble bonding with any of our guests when they ask to meet the Fairy Tails dogs," Megan told him.

"They just need to spend a little time getting to know him," Jake said as he rubbed Barnaby's belly.

"Hard to do when they only get to spend a few minutes with him. He takes a while to warm up to people." She paused. "He loves you, though. You just said he'd make a great barn dog. Maybe you should give him a try."

"Whoa," Jake said as he stood. He remembered mentioning the possibility of getting a barn dog once a while ago, but he hadn't really thought about it since. "I don't know about that."

"I'm not trying to pressure you or anything." She walked over and placed a hand on his arm. "I was just watching you play with him, and it hit me how comfortable he is with you, compared to the way he acts around the potential adopters who come by the castle. Anyway, if you wanted to try him out, you totally could. Just keep him at your house for a few days, see what you think. He'd still be our foster dog, and if you don't want to keep him, you can just give him back to me."

He grinned at her. "He's already practically lived at my house for the last month."

"Yeah, but I was usually the one caring for him, and he came back to the castle with Chandler and me every morning. Anyway, just something to think about." She turned to leave, calling to Barnaby to follow her. He trotted after her, his leash dragging on the barn floor.

"You know what? Let him stay with me tonight and see what happens."

"Really?" She paused in the doorway of the barn, looking over her shoulder at him.

"Yeah. But if anyone's interested in adopting him in the meantime, don't hold him back on my account."

She was nodding and smiling. "And I'll bring him with me to the Spring Fling, unless you tell me not to."

"Let's not get ahead of ourselves." He stooped to pick up Barnaby's leash, and the dog moved obediently toward him, tail wagging. "Will I see you tonight, or will it just be me and Barnaby?"

"I wish I could, but I promised Elle and Ruby I'd help with prep for the festival. Apparently, we've got brochures to fold or some similarly exciting activity." She rolled her eyes good-naturedly. "Wine will be involved, I'm sure."

"I'll leave you ladies to it, then. You'll give me a chance to catch up on my word count."

"How close are you to finishing?" she asked.

"I've got two chapters left to write, but these last scenes usually go really fast. I might even finish tonight if I pull a late night."

"Now you'll have someone to keep you company." She leaned in for a quick kiss. "Text me later?"

"Count on it." He watched her walk away before turning to look down at the dog at his side. "You and me tonight, buddy. Guys' night."

Barnaby stared at him, blonde tail swooshing in the dirt, a slightly confused look in his eyes.

"I know, this is weird for me too. Guess we'll figure it out together, okay?" He finished up in the barn and headed for the house. Barnaby trotted along quietly beside him. There was already a dish of water in his kitchen and a small bag of dog food in his pantry from the many times Megan had brought her foster dogs with her to spend the night. In fact, there was even a package of treats on the counter. He pulled one of them out and tossed it to Barnaby before popping open a beer for himself.

"We're going to spend the afternoon in here," he told Barnaby as he walked down the hall to the office. "Not very exciting, but if you get bored, just make a nuisance of yourself and we'll ask Megan to take you back to the castle, okay?"

He sat at the desk and opened his laptop. Barnaby watched for a moment and then lay down on the floor nearby.

"I'll get you something to lay on next time I'm up," Jake told him absently, but Barnaby didn't seem to mind the hardwood floor. He'd spread himself out in a patch of sunlight and was already sound asleep.

Jake opened his manuscript, familiarized himself with where he'd left off, and settled in to write. He hadn't been exaggerating when he told Megan these last chapters tended to come fast. His main character, Derrick, was closing in on the killer, and all hell was about to break loose. Soon, the only sound in the office was the clatter of Jake's fingers over the keys and an occasional snore from Barnaby. The next thing Jake knew, the sun hung low in the sky, and he only had one chapter left to write.

"You're not bad company," he told the dog as he stood to stretch his legs. Actually, he'd enjoyed the company. Sometimes, he would talk out loud to himself while he was figuring out a scene, and Barnaby had made a great sounding board, all pricked ears and wagging tail, no interrupting chatter or any of the distractions a human companion posed while he was writing. He'd always written in solitude, but this…this he could get used to.

Maybe.

He led the way into the kitchen for refreshments. Since it was dinnertime, he poured some kibble into Barnaby's bowl and then heated up a pre-packaged meal for himself, something he'd become quite adept at over the years.

Over the last month, though, he'd gotten used to home-cooked meals here with Megan at his side. He'd gotten used to a lot of things where she was concerned. He and Barnaby shared dinner before walking down to the barn to check on the horses. Bug and Dusty were out in the riding ring, but Twister and Duchess were in the barn, where he'd left them while he did some work on the fencing earlier. No doubt they were eager to get out to their pastures for the night.

Barnaby had accompanied Jake in the barn without his leash in the past. The dog had good recall. So, he unclipped him now and let him follow Jake into the barn to get Twister. If Barnaby misbehaved in any way, Twister wouldn't be bothered by it. But Barnaby stayed a respectable distance away as Jake led the horse out to his pasture. All the same, he put Barnaby in an empty stall while he brought Duchess out. That horse was too valuable to take any risks with.

Jake's pulse kicked up as he thought of his meeting with Mr. Nichols on Monday. If he was impressed, it could really help launch Jake's career, and frankly, he needed the boost. Training one horse at a time wasn't sustainable. He needed at least two to live comfortably and hoped to expand that number in the future. But, first things first. With Barnaby in tow, he headed back to the farmhouse to finish writing the book.

MEGAN HAD HARDLY SEEN JAKE—OR Barnaby—over the past two days. She, Ruby, and Elle had been so busy up at the castle getting ready for the Spring Fling festival that she hadn't had much time for anything else. But she and Jake had texted regularly, and he seemed content having Barnaby with him.

It was strange for Megan, not having a dog in her room the last two nights. Quiet. It was nice not to have to take care of anyone furry for a change, though. She'd never had a dog before coming to the castle, and their foster dogs were a big responsibility. She wasn't complaining about it, but she wasn't complaining about having a few nights off either.

On Saturday morning, she, Ruby, and Elle were down at the field behind the Towering Pines downtown area bright and early. Already, it had been transformed into a festival. There were carnival rides and food stands, and along the far edge of the field, vendors were setting up their tables. Mountains rolled behind them, green and lush. It promised to be a beautiful mid-April day, already warm and sunny despite the early hour.

Megan reached automatically for her camera, crouching against the dewy grass to snap a series of photos of the rides silhouetted against the mountains and sky while Ruby and Elle went ahead to walk the dogs around the field before things got busy.

"Working already?"

She turned at the sound of Jake's voice, pressing one knee into the grass to keep her balance. "The planning committee hired me to be the official photographer for the day."

"No kidding?" He smiled down at her, and her heart swooped right into her ribs. Barnaby stood at his side, and the sight of man and dog together made her all warm and mushy inside.

She aimed the camera in his direction and snapped,

capturing him against the background of the festival. Then, she stood. "Yeah. Priya recommended me, apparently. And who am I to turn down a fun gig like this one?"

"That's great." He took her free hand in his, tugging her up against him. "Your photography business seems to really be taking off."

"It helps that I have the most beautiful location in town at my fingertips for sessions."

"Also helps that you're ridiculously talented." His mouth covered hers.

She closed her eyes, breathing in his scent, absorbing the feel of his lips and the way his hands cradled her waist, sure and strong. She'd come to Virginia on a whim, hoping for a little excitement to shake up her life. When they first found out they'd won *Modern Home and Gardens'* Almost Royal contest, she hadn't taken any of it seriously. Moving into a castle owned by a member of the British aristocracy? It was absolute insanity, but Megan was always up for a good adventure.

So, she'd come, hoping for a few months of fun, never expecting to stay. She hadn't expected Virginia—or Rosemont Castle—to feel like home, or to discover a new level of closeness with the women who'd been her best friends since childhood. She hadn't expected to be scarred in a car accident right as all her dreams were coming to fruition.

And she had never expected to fall in love with this man who was everything and nothing she'd ever imagined having or needing. Jake had snuck past all her defenses and settled that part of her that had always been restless and searching, always ready to move on to the next better thing. She couldn't imagine finding anything or anyone better than Jake Reardon.

"Missed you," she murmured between kisses.

"I didn't go anywhere." Amusement laced his tone.

"You know what I mean." She smiled against his lips. "Haven't seen you in two days, you or Barnaby. It's been awfully lonely in my bed."

"Been lonely in mine too, although Barnaby seems to think your side of the bed is his now."

"I can't quite picture you two sharing a bed," she admitted, glancing down at the dog, who lay in the grass beside them, taking in the bustle of festival preparations.

"Wasn't my idea, and I'm hoping you'll be there to kick him out tonight."

"I was planning on it." She crouched down to say hi to Barnaby. "You don't mind if I join you in Jake's bed tonight, do you?"

Barnaby crawled forward in the grass, tail doing full loop-de-loops as he kissed her face.

"That looks like a yes to me," Jake said.

"What are you doing all day?" she asked, looking up at him while she rubbed Barnaby.

"Just hanging out, mostly. Hoping to see a few potential clients, put some feelers out there about my business, that kind of thing. Thanks for letting me put my brochures on your table."

"Of course." She stood, leading the way toward Rosemont Castle's table. "Feel free to send anyone who's interested in your work our way. We'll sing your praises while we hand out brochures."

"They look great, by the way," he said. "The brochures. They're about a thousand percent nicer than anything I imagined having for myself."

"I just took the photos." She looked down at the stack of brochures on the table. The cover was a full color shot of Jake with Duchess. He looked handsome, professional, and competent, and the horse could have been a model. "Ruby laid out the brochure for you."

"Well, between the two of you, my fledging business looks like a million bucks, and I can't thank you enough."

"It was my pleasure." She pressed another kiss to his lips. "And Ruby was happy to do her part too. You did us a big favor working with Bug and Dusty this month, and this was the least we could do to repay you."

"Hopefully they'll find homes soon."

"Actually," she said, "I heard someone might be interested in Dusty. Priya was going to try to set up a time for her to come out and meet and ride Dusty next week."

"Great news."

Elle and Ruby walked up then with the rest of their foster dogs. Barnaby scampered over to greet them, his leash tugging against Megan's fingers.

"I'll let you guys finish getting ready, then," Jake said. "Do you need anything?"

"Unless you can magically make coffee appear, no," Elle said with a slightly wan smile, "but thank you for asking."

"Actually, I think there's a tent over there with coffee for the vendors. Want me to go get some?" Jake gestured toward a blue tent at the edge of the field, where a line waited.

"I was just joking," Elle said, "but if they really have coffee over there and you don't mind getting us some, we'll love you forever."

Megan felt her cheeks heat, as though Elle's words somehow projected the feelings running rampant through her since she'd seen Jake this morning. But of course, Elle was just joking. Jake headed off toward the coffee tent.

"What's that funny face for?" Ruby asked, waving a hand in Megan's direction as she set down a bowl for the dogs and began filling it from the jug of water beneath their table.

"What face?" Megan moved around behind the table with Barnaby.

"The face that said, 'oh shit, Elle just said the L word to Jake,'" Ruby said.

"What?" Elle rubbed at her brow, apparently slow on the uptake before she'd had caffeine. "Oh, because I said—" Her eyes widened comically. "Oh."

"So, are you trying to tell us something?" Ruby asked. "And have you told Jake?"

"No, and no," Megan said stubbornly, dropping into her seat. "You're being ridiculous."

"So, you don't love him?" Ruby grinned, equally stubborn.

Elle watched quietly, a hand pressed over her mouth in obvious delight.

Megan rolled her eyes. "Maybe I do, but this is just casual, and whatever. We'll see what happens."

"Um, this is kind of huge news," Ruby said. "I mean, unless I'm mistaken, you've never been in love before."

"No, I haven't," she admitted, staring down at Barnaby, who'd curled up at her feet. "But it doesn't have to be a big deal, I mean, does it?"

"It's a big deal," Elle confirmed. "But in a good way, because Jake looks pretty smitten too, and really, you guys seem perfect for each other. You've been so happy since you started dating him. You seem, I don't know...settled or something, but again, in a good way."

Megan didn't say anything. She knew exactly what Elle meant, because she felt settled...in a good way. But she also knew it wasn't as simple as that. "Jake's still healing."

"That's true," Ruby said. "But it doesn't mean he doesn't love you too."

"All the same, I'm not going to say anything just yet," Megan said. "We're in a really good place right now. I don't want to make things more complicated than they need to be."

"In my experience," Elle said. "It's always good to tell someone you love them. As Jake knows better than most anyone, tomorrow isn't guaranteed."

Megan rested a hand on Elle's shoulder as she registered the depth of her words. "I'll play it by ear."

From there, the morning got busy. Priya arrived at the table beside theirs with a host of volunteers, dogs on leashes, and cats in crates. The fairgrounds started to fill in as early birds arrived to get a head start on the day. Jake swung by with a carrier of coffee and a quick kiss for Megan before heading off into the growing crowd.

The rescue pets attracted a lot of attention, and they had a steady stream of people visiting their table. She saw Priya handing out lots of adoption applications, and the donation jar on the table was already half full by mid-morning.

"What's his name?" a woman asked, bending down to let Barnaby sniff her hand.

"Barnaby," Megan told her, feeling something catch in her chest at the idea of him being adopted. She'd adopted out over a dozen foster dogs at this point, but somehow she'd become attached to this one, or at least attached to the idea of Jake keeping him. "He's a three-year-old pit mix, very shy with new people, but he warms right up once he gets to know you."

Barnaby shuffled closer to Megan's chair, pressing himself against her leg.

"Aww, he's a sweetie," the woman said. "He reminds me of a dog my parents had when I was a kid. What's the adoption process like?"

"Well, you'd need to grab one of those applications." She pointed to the stack on the shelter's table. "Barnaby's being fostered with us at Rosemont Castle, so once the shelter approves you to adopt, you could come out to the castle and spend time with him there to make sure he's the right dog for you."

"It would be nice to get the chance to hang out with him like that," she said. "I'm definitely going to put in an application. I've been wanting to stop by the shelter and look for a dog, but coming out to Rosemont Castle sounds more fun."

"It does, right?" Megan smiled at her. "There's no guarantee Barnaby will still be available, but the sooner you get your application in, the better. And if he's gone, I'll have someone new for you to meet."

"Okay, I'm filling out my application right now." The

woman rubbed Barnaby and blew him a kiss before moving over to the shelter's table.

"I need to head out and take some photos," Megan told Ruby. "Do you want to keep him here at the table for me?"

"You got it." Ruby took Barnaby's leash from her.

Megan ruffled his furry head before she stood and headed into the crowd. This was the part of today she'd been most looking forward to. Camera in hand, she moved through the festival, capturing happy details as well as the overall look of the event. She snapped a little girl taking a big bite of her cotton candy, pink fluff stuck to her nose, and a couple on the Ferris wheel, sharing a kiss as they swooped overhead.

"Want to take a ride?" Jake said from behind her.

"You've got an uncanny ability to find me in a crowd," she said, turning to face him.

"Not hard when you stand out in any crowd." He reached out to cup her cheek, a look of pure, unabashed affection in his eyes. "Also, the big camera helps."

"Ha." She punched his biceps playfully.

"So, want to ride the Ferris wheel with me?"

She opened her mouth to say no, because she was working right now, but on second thought… "Actually, I could get some great overhead shots of the fair from up there."

"You can call it work, but I just want to make out with my girlfriend in one of those baskets." Jake winked at her.

"Well, in that case…" She grabbed his hand, leading him toward the line for the ride. "Have you got tickets?"

He held up a strip of them. "I was hoping I might convince you to have a little fun with me."

"A man who plans for success. I like that."

They held hands, laughing and chatting as they waited in line. Megan felt relaxed and happy with Jake at her side, and when they finally made their way into a little green basket, she settled close to him on the seat.

"Not afraid of heights, are you?" he asked.

"Nope. I went sky diving on my twenty first birthday."

"Damn." He looked at her, his expression equal parts impressed and aroused. "I don't know why the image of you jumping out of an airplane is turning me on, but it definitely is."

"It's the adrenaline rush," she whispered as their basket lurched forward.

"I do love a good adrenaline rush." He leaned in and pressed his lips against hers.

"Yeah? What else do you do for a rush?" she asked, squeezing his hand.

"I think I've lived for a long time with insufficient adrenaline," he said softly. "You've changed that for me."

"Happy to help." Their kiss turned more urgent then, tongues teasing as the basket slowly made its way toward the top, stopping and starting as the Ferris wheel was loaded with new passengers. Finally, they broke apart, desperate for oxygen.

"I'd like to discover more new things this year," Jake said. "Want to help me?"

"I'd love to." And there was that damn word again. "What did you have in mind?"

"I don't know. Anything. Everything. I'd jump out of an airplane with you." He stared at the fairgrounds laid out beneath them. "I'd also like to take a trip, even just a small one while I get my business off the ground. I haven't left Towering Pines in too long."

"I'm totally game for that. I love to travel. Hold that thought for a minute, though." Their basket had come to a stop at the top of the wheel, and this would be her best chance to take photos before they started moving in earnest. Securing the strap around herself, she lifted the camera and started snapping, capturing the festival laid out beneath them.

The basket lurched as it began to move, and she put the camera away, reaching on instinct for her phone. She held it out and snapped a selfie of them, snuggled up next to each other with the blur of the fairgrounds behind them, carefree smiles on their faces. She leaned in to press a kiss against his cheek, snapping another selfie as she did so, not even noticing that she had turned the scarred side of her face toward the camera.

## 15

_____

"Ice cream?" Jake asked Megan as they strolled past the row of food trucks. They'd just finished eating an early lunch of chicken and waffles, a staple of his upbringing that Megan had never experienced before.

"I never say no to ice cream," she said with a smile. "But then I've got to get back to the table so Elle and Ruby can take a break and have some fun too."

"Want me to sit with you while they're gone?"

"Sure." She gave him a sweet smile that seemed to melt something inside his chest. Or maybe it was something in his knees, because he felt a little wobbly as he stared into the sparkling depths of her cinnamon eyes. "Your brochures are on our table, after all."

He led the way toward the ice cream stand, which miraculously didn't have much of a line.

She gripped his hand. "Oh look, it's the kind where they dip your cone in that chocolate shell."

He loved this side of her, the happy, carefree woman who forgot to hide her face behind the curtain of her hair. "I haven't had that since I was a kid."

"It's my absolute favorite."

They made their way to the front of the line and ordered two chocolate-dipped cones, which they licked as they crossed the field toward the vendor tables to relieve Ruby and Elle.

"Oh, I meant to tell you," Megan said, grinning as he swiped a dot of ice cream off her nose. "There was a woman at our table this morning who was interested in Barnaby. Who knows if she'll follow through, but if you're interested in him, you should let me know soon."

"Hmm." He crunched through the chocolate shell, taking a big bite of his ice cream. These things were messier to eat than he remembered. Already, he had melted ice cream running over his hand. "I hadn't really given it much thought yet."

"I figured you hadn't, but just a heads up."

"Thanks." His gut reaction was to tell her to let the woman go ahead and adopt Barnaby if she followed through. But he'd enjoyed the company the last few days. Barnaby was a quiet, well-behaved dog, maybe just what he was looking for in a barn companion. "I'll let you know."

"Okay." She gave his hand a squeeze.

"Jake!"

He turned at the familiar voice to find the Robertsons walking toward them, and a funny feeling raced through his gut, replacing the usual pleasure of seeing them with something much more...uncomfortable. Because even though he'd talked to them about his relationship with Megan, introducing them to her definitely felt awkward.

But there was no way around it now. Thankfully, Tina saved the moment as she was so good at. "You must be Megan," she said warmly, extending a hand. "I'm Tina Robertson, and this is my husband, Walt."

"Of course," Megan said. "It's nice to meet you. Jake's told me so much about you both."

"Likewise." Tina abandoned her handshake and pulled Megan in for a gentle hug. "He's like family to us."

Megan darted a glance in his direction. "I know it must be

hard to see him with someone else."

"It is." Tina's smile fell, her eyes going glossy. "Alana couldn't have asked for a more loving and devoted husband. We're so blessed to have him in our lives."

Jake felt an uncomfortable squeeze in his chest. After his own turbulent childhood, he wasn't sure where he'd be today if he hadn't met the Robertsons. "That feeling is definitely mutual."

"I haven't seen you at church," Walt said to Megan. "Have you found a place to worship since you moved to Towering Pines?"

"I'm Jewish," she told him. "And yes, I've visited the nearest synagogue, although it's a bit of a drive from Towering Pines. Everyone has been very welcoming."

"Glad to hear it," Walt said with a polite smile.

"Well, we won't keep you guys," Tina said. "But I'm so glad we bumped into you."

"It was great to see you," Jake told her.

"You too, honey." She pulled him in for a brief hug, and then they were on their way.

"That went surprisingly well," Megan said, returning her attention to her half-melted ice cream as they started walking again.

"It's not surprising if you know them. They're pretty great people."

"I'm glad you have them," she said. "And I'm glad to have met them."

They made their way back to the table and took over for Ruby and Elle, who headed off into the crowd for lunch and a break. He and Megan finished their ice cream cones and rinsed their hands from the jug of water under the table for the dogs. Barnaby settled at his feet, tail thumping happily against the grass.

"You know, maybe I will put in an adoption application for him," Jake said, surprising even himself. Maybe it was time for someone—or something—permanent in his life, and Barnaby seemed like a good place to start.

"Well, spoiler alert, but I have some pull at the shelter," Megan told him with a delighted grin. "So, if you want him, he's yours. In fact, we can tell Priya right now if you want." She gestured toward the woman sitting at the next table, speaking to a family with two small children who were fawning over a gray and white spotted cat in a cage.

Jake looked down at the dog at his feet. "Yeah, you know, why not? He's proved his skills as a farm dog the last few days, and he's good company too. I'd be glad to call him mine."

∿

IT WAS LATE by the time they made it back to the castle, and Megan was exhausted, but it was the good kind of tired, the kind that left a smile on her face, no matter how weary.

"Stay over tonight?" Jake asked as his truck approached the fork in the drive separating the farmhouse from the main castle.

"Yeah." She had enough of her things stashed at his place now that it was an easy decision logistically, and after spending two nights alone in her bed at the castle, she was craving his company tonight. "I'd like that."

"So would I." He reached over and gripped her thigh, his fingers warm and strong. A thrill ran through her system at the contact. Yeah, it had been too long since she'd been in his bed. Two nights too long.

Which meant, what? She wanted to spend every night in Jake's bed? She swallowed over the uncomfortable realization, because she was a woman who liked her space, her independence. Apparently, love made her a clingy sap.

"You okay?" he asked as he pulled up in front of the farmhouse.

"Just tired." She pressed her hand over his.

"It was a long day."

"A big day for this guy." She turned to look at Barnaby, who was passed out on the backseat. "I guess getting adopted is exhausting."

"You'll need two new foster dogs now."

"Yeah." That thought was somewhat exhausting too. Constantly bringing in new dogs to foster was equal parts exciting and overwhelming. The new dogs always took time to adjust. But then, she looked at Barnaby again. She'd never gotten to see this part before, one of her foster dogs after his or her adoption. It filled her heart with warmth. This was exactly what they'd set out to accomplish with their Fairy Tails program. "I'm glad I'll still get to see Barnaby around. He's a great dog."

"He is. But he's not the only one I'm glad to have around." He squeezed her fingers.

"No?" she asked, hating the neediness she heard in her voice.

"I've grown pretty fond of you both, in case you hadn't noticed."

"I noticed," she whispered.

He parked the truck in front of the farmhouse. When they made it inside, Jake pushed her up against the wall in the hallway, his lips covering hers. "Missed this."

"It's only been two days," she breathed, her breasts pressed against the firm wall of his chest.

"Two very long days." He gripped her ass, angling her hips so that they met his, letting her feel how much he'd missed her. "Missed you in my bed."

"Is that all?" She gasped as he nipped at her neck.

He drew back to stare into her eyes, his expression serious even as his eyes blazed with heat. "Not nearly all. I missed you in my arms, on my couch, at the breakfast table. I missed talking to you and looking at your photos and hearing about your day."

"Oh." Her heart did some kind of acrobatics in her chest that left her dizzy. "I thought you might enjoy some peace and quiet."

"I've had all the peace and quiet I want for this lifetime." His hands slid beneath her shirt, skimming up her back to the hook of her bra. "It would suit me just fine if you wanted to move the rest of your stuff down here to the farmhouse."

"Wait. What?" She froze, her eyes locked on his.

He bent his head to kiss her, his lips pressing firmly against hers. "Move in with me."

"I—"

"If you want to, of course," he said, continuing to kiss her as his hands unhooked her bra and swept around to palm her breasts. "But I'd love to have you and Barnaby here with me all the time."

"I don't know what to say."

"Just think about it." His thumbs slid over her nipples, his rough skin creating the most beautiful friction that had her boneless with need.

*Move in with me.*

She'd never lived with a man before, never even really considered it. But this man...

He lifted her, carrying her to the couch, where he lowered her to the leather upholstery, pressing her into it as he worked open her jeans, hands and mouth everywhere. To think he was a virgin last month. Now, he handled her with confidence and expertise as he stroked her with his fingers before sheathing himself in a condom.

"Yes," she moaned as he pushed inside.

"You got it, baby." He withdrew and thrust again, filling her completely. "Anything you want. Everything you want."

"Yes," she said again, eyes sliding shut with pleasure, not sure if she was answering his question or just responding to his touch. Maybe both.

"One of my favorite words," he growled, hips beginning to

move in a steady rhythm as his hands continued to work her body. "So good. Fuck, yes."

She melted into the upholstery as desire built inside her, a smile curving her lips at his commentary. Jake was talkative during sex, vocal about his pleasure, and she loved it, loved every single thing about him. They moved together sloppily, hands grasping as they both drew closer to their release. She gripped his ass, attempting to draw him even deeper inside her.

"I've got you," he murmured, bringing one of his hands between them to stroke her clit as his hips pounded into her.

"Yes." And then she was coming. Tears leaked from her eyes as release washed through her, causing her whole body to tense and then go limp beneath him.

Jake groaned as he found his own release. "Can't get enough of this." He dropped his head, his lips meeting hers for a messy kiss. "Can't get enough of you."

"I love you." The words tumbled out without her permission, and her body went from limp with pleasure to tense in the span of one frantic beat of her heart.

Jake froze, his brown eyes meeting hers, questions swirling in their languid depths.

"I mean, I'd love to move in with you," she said quickly, but it did nothing to negate what she'd already said.

He was silent for a long time, chest heaving against hers, one hand beneath her ass, the other braced against the couch. "I love you too."

All the air rushed from her lungs. "What?"

He rolled them so he could lay beside her. "I hadn't really thought about it yet, but I do. It's why this house felt so empty and lonely the last two days. I love being with you every moment of the day because I love you, Megan."

"Oh." More tears slid over her cheeks, and she swiped at them with the palm of her hand as Jake drew her closer against him.

"Definitely wasn't expecting to hear those words from you

tonight," he murmured. "Especially after you balked at moving in with me."

"I didn't balk," she whispered, closing her eyes against the emotions welling up inside her. What was happening? How had they gone from a fun day at the fair to him asking her to move in with him and her blurting out that she loved him?

"So, is that a yes, then?" His hand stroked her hair.

"Yes." She opened her eyes, meeting his. "I'll move in with you."

His lips curved in a wide smile. "You just made me a very happy man."

"Really?" Her brain was definitely operating at a slower speed than her mouth tonight.

"Really. Don't move." He hitched his jeans into place and walked into the bathroom.

She'd almost forgotten they were still mostly dressed and crammed together on the couch in the living room. She righted her own clothes and then Jake was back. He scooped her effortlessly into his arms and carried her to the bedroom. Barnaby followed, tail wagging. He settled onto a large dog bed in the corner.

"A dog bed?" Megan asked, heart melting that Jake had already started buying him things before he'd even adopted him.

"Helps to keep him out of mine," he told her before cracking another smile. "But he still winds up here at some point during the night."

She blinked up at him, seeing their future so clearly, living and working together here at Rosemont Castle, sharing this bed every night. It was everything she could have ever imagined for herself, so why did the thought terrify her? Everything was happening so fast. Too fast? Had Jake really finished healing? Had she?

～

JAKE SAT astride Duchess as she moved around the ring at an easy jog. Mr. Nichols watched from the other side of the fence, phone held high as he recorded a video to send his daughter. The horse moved briskly, ears pricked, eager and excited to be working in the ring. He nudged her with his heels, lifting the reins, and she broke into a lope. The sound of her hooves drumming against the hard-packed earth filled his ears.

She made his job easy. Too easy? He did enjoy the thrill of a more challenging horse, but right now, she was making him look good in front of a client, and he really couldn't complain about that. After a few minutes, Mr. Nichols put the phone away and leaned against the fence, a satisfied smile on his face.

Jake eased Duchess to a walk and approached him. "What do you think?"

"I think she's one of the most gorgeous creatures I've ever seen, and you've done a fine job with her," Mr. Nichols said.

"Thank you. It helps having a horse like Duchess to work with." Jake leaned down to rub her neck, and Duchess bobbed her head enthusiastically. "I think she's ready to move to your barn, with me returning for a series of training sessions while Kassie rides her, as we discussed."

"I agree," Mr. Nichols said with a nod. "I'll arrange for her transport this week. Are you looking for more work?"

"I am," Jake said, feeling his posture straighten in anticipation of whatever his client might be about to offer. He desperately needed more work, and a referral from Mr. Nichols could be invaluable.

A series of loud, sharp barks rang out across the field, followed by a scream, and then Bug was running straight toward them, lead line trailing from her halter, bouncing off her flank and further frightening her. Jake had been peripherally aware that Megan was in the process of bringing Bug into the barn, as she often did, but something had obviously gone wrong. A vise clamped over his chest as he remembered her scream.

"Whoa, Bug," he called to the panicked horse, his attention divided between her and Duchess, who fidgeted nervously beneath him. Duchess was a solid horse, but she was young and green, and Bug's alarm could easily become contagious. "Easy, girl. Easy, Duchess," he murmured, shifting in the saddle to keep himself centered as she danced sideways.

Mr. Nichols flattened himself against the fence as Bug raced closer. Jake guided Duchess toward the center of the ring, talking soothingly to her as her ears flicked in unease. Megan came around the corner of the barn, looking stricken but—as far as he could see—unharmed. *Thank God.* At the last moment, Bug dodged to the side, avoiding collision with the fence, and galloped down the lane toward the main castle.

"There you go," Jake murmured to Duchess. "Nothing to worry about. You okay?" he called to Megan.

She nodded, hands clasped around her waist. "One of Elle's foster dogs got loose and scared Bug, and she bolted. I couldn't hold on to her."

"Okay. Don't panic." He dismounted Duchess and led her toward the fence. "She probably hasn't gone far. Let me get Duchess settled, and we'll go find her."

"I can handle Duchess," Mr. Nichols said, stepping forward, "if you want to go after your runaway horse."

Jake hesitated. Duchess was Mr. Nichols's horse after all. He owned several other horses, and although he generally had staff who helped him in the barn, Jake didn't doubt the man could cool down and untack a horse if necessary. Duchess would be fine with him, except it still made Jake feel somewhat inadequate to hand her off like this, especially when Mr. Nichols had been on the verge of offering him a referral for a new client. He extended the reins. "I appreciate that. Thank you."

"Not a problem. I'd enjoy spending some time with her." Mr. Nichols took his horse and led her toward the barn.

With that taken care of, Jake went to the feed room for a

bucket and some grain and then strode after Megan in the direction Bug had gone. Irritation rose inside him, not directed at Megan, but at the situation in general. Hopefully he hadn't lost his shot with Mr. Nichols. He caught up with her halfway up the lane, cheeks flushed, jogging toward the castle.

"I'm so sorry," she huffed, looking at him over her shoulder.

"No need to be. There's no holding on to a horse when they bolt. They outweigh you by over a thousand pounds. If you'd tried, you might have been dragged." He put a hand on her arm, tugging gently. "Slow down. You can't run as fast as she can, and you'll have better luck catching her if you're calm when we find her."

"How far do you think she went?" Megan asked, slowing to a walk beside him.

"There's no telling, but probably not far." He started shaking the grain bucket, hoping to entice Bug back on her own. "Horses are flight animals. They run when they're frightened, but as long as the dog didn't chase her, she's probably grazing somewhere on the grounds right now."

"He didn't chase her," Megan told him. "Elle took him back to the castle as soon as she saw what happened."

"That's good," Jake said. "Don't worry. Horses get loose fairly often, just like dogs."

"We had a foster dog once who ran off for two days and turned up miles away from the castle," Megan told him, her expression earnest.

"Well, let's hope Bug isn't that ambitious. In fact..." He pointed to the field ahead, where Bug stood grazing contentedly in the sunshine.

"Oh, thank God," Megan murmured. "Do you think she'll let us catch her?"

"I sure do. She doesn't generally play hard to catch. The trick is not to remind her that she has the freedom to run off. Just approach with confidence." He walked right up to Bug, rubbing her neck as offered her a handful of grain before reaching down to grab her lead shank. "Hey there, girl."

"Phew." Megan joined him beside Bug. "You gave me quite a scare." She rubbed the horse, and Bug nuzzled her affectionately.

"She's gotten pretty fond of you," Jake observed.

"The feeling is mutual." Megan took the lead from his hand, guiding Bug confidently down the lane toward the barn. The horse looked like a different animal than the one who'd arrived a month and a half ago, skinny, ragged, and covered in dog bites. The wounds had healed now, leaving fresh pink scars against her dappled white coat. "She'll be sad if Dusty gets adopted tomorrow, I think."

"She might be, yeah," he agreed. "They're nicely bonded. It's too bad the adopter isn't interested in the pair of them."

"It is." Megan looked up at Bug's face. "I hope she'll be okay."

"She will be. She's pretty resilient. Most animals are," he commented. "People too."

Megan glanced over at him with a smile. "I suppose that's true."

Yesterday, she'd brought down the rest of her things from the castle. Maybe it should feel like a big deal that he was living with a woman for the first time in his life. Probably, it should. But it didn't. Everything with Megan felt easy and comfortable, like he'd been waiting his whole life for it. He hadn't put a label on it, but as soon as she'd blurted out her declaration of love last night, he knew he felt the same way.

He loved her. It was a different kind of love than he'd felt for Alana, a deeper, more mature love. The kind of love that demanded nothing but offered everything. With Megan at his side, the world felt lighter and brighter, full of all the warm, wonderful things he'd watched other people experience for so much of his life.

"I can take her from here if you need to get back to your client," Megan said as they approached the barn. Dusty whinnied from her stall, and Bug returned her call, head up and ears pricked, her step quickening as she approached her friend.

"All right. Holler if you need any help." He knew she'd be fine, but he kept an eye on her all the same. Jake could only hope he'd be fine too, because he'd been on the verge of earning Mr. Nichols' seal of approval before he'd run off and left him with Duchess. Not ideal, to say the least.

"Oh, good," Mr. Nichols said as he walked out of the barn, smiling at them. "Glad she didn't go too far."

"So am I," Megan told him with a warm smile. "Sorry for losing her in the first place and interrupting you and Jake during your training session."

"Not at all," Mr. Nichols told her. "It gave me a chance to spend a little time with Duchess, and to see Jake in action."

"I have yet to see him get flustered, and these rescue horses have given us plenty of trouble," she said as she led Bug into her stall. "Jake always knows exactly what to do."

He rocked back on his heels, hands shoved into the pockets of his jeans. "I wouldn't say I always know what to do, but this is my job, after all."

"I have to agree with Megan," Mr. Nichols said. "I was impressed with how calmly you handled everything just now. A friend of mine has a horse he's looking for some help with. She's a scraper, among other things."

"A what?" Megan furrowed her brow as she closed and latched Bug's stall door.

"She takes riders under low-hanging branches to try to get rid of them," Mr. Nichols explained with a smile. "You up for a job like that, Jake?"

"Absolutely. I've had plenty of experience with difficult horses."

Mr. Nichols clapped him on the shoulder. "I'll put in a good word for you."

"Thank you, sir. I appreciate that." With any luck, he was on the cusp of bigger and better things, on several fronts.

## 16

$O$ ver the next week, Megan settled into the farmhouse with Jake. She brought home two new foster dogs—a pair of little black and white Havanese mixes named Oreo and Cookie. Barnaby ignored the new arrivals for the most part, seeming to think they were too small to be actual dogs. She was confident they would be adopted quickly, once she'd had the chance to show them off to the castle's guests. They were small, adorable, and well-behaved, exactly the kind of dog that seemed most popular in the Fairy Tails program.

She worked at the castle during the day and spent her free time down at the barn with Jake and the horses. Duchess had gone home, and Rumor—the new horse he was training—had arrived to take her place. This one was giving Jake a run for his money, but Megan had no doubt he'd get him straightened out in the end.

On Thursday, Dusty Star was adopted. She and Bug whinnied to each other as the trailer pulled down the drive, and Megan felt a pang of sadness to see Dusty go, especially for Bug's sake. But Dusty had been adopted by an experienced equine family with two other horses who often went on trail rides. It was the perfect home for her. She'd be loved, well cared for, and ridden regularly. Bug, who wasn't yet able to be ridden, was going to be harder to place.

"She'll be okay," Jake said as he walked up behind Megan, who was watching Bug pace in the riding ring. "I'll move Twister to the pasture next to hers so he can help keep her company."

"I feel bad for her," Megan admitted, leaning back against Jake.

"Because she's missing Dusty right now?" he asked. "Or because of her history?"

"Both," she said softly, her gaze settling on the bright pink scar just above Bug's muzzle.

"She doesn't know she's scarred." Jake's hands settled on her shoulders, warm and comforting. She sucked in a breath as that familiar hot, prickly sensation crept over the left side of her face. "She only knows that dogs can sometimes be scary and that—right now, but probably not for much longer—she's missing her friend. Anyway, I have a strong feeling that things are about to turn around for Bug, just the way they have for us."

She looked over her shoulder at him. "You do?"

He nodded. "And to that end, I'm going to start working in the ring with her this weekend. She's watched me work with the other horses. I think she's ready to learn herself. She's a curious horse with a strong spirit. Those are good qualities."

Megan felt herself relax against him. Somehow, everything seemed to make sense when he said it. Maybe spending so much time with horses had allowed him to see the world through the same kind of clarifying lens they did. Because he had an uncanny ability to filter out bullshit and get right to the heart of the matter. It was one of the reasons she'd fallen in love with him.

"Are you finished at the castle for the night?" he asked.

"Mm hmm."

"Want to help me finish up here in the barn? Then I thought

maybe we could go into town for dinner. I have a craving for Nonna's fried chicken."

"Sounds perfect." She wasn't exactly sure when she'd become a woman who enjoyed helping in the barn and spending every free moment with her man, but here she was. While he went to get Twister, she clipped a lead on Bug and brought her out to her pasture. The little horse walked beside her with an urgency in her step, as if she might find Dusty waiting for her outside. "We'll find you a new buddy soon," Megan told her.

"Maybe sooner than you think," Jake said from behind her.

"Really? Who?"

"I have someone coming out this weekend who's interested in boarding his horse here. It took me longer than I expected to find boarders, but hopefully that's about to change."

"You've been busy this week," she commented as she led Bug into her pasture and closed the gate behind her.

"I have. Lots of exciting things on the horizon." He put Twister in the pasture next to Bug's, and the two horses trotted over to greet each other.

Megan and Jake finished up in the barn and headed to the farmhouse to walk the dogs before dinner.

"You know, for someone who's never been that much of an animal person, I sure do have a lot of them in my life right now," Megan commented as she clipped leashes onto Oreo and Cookie.

"That's true. Too many?"

"Not necessarily." She looked down at the fluffy little dogs at her feet. "No, I like having them around."

After all the creatures were cared for, she and Jake went into town for dinner, managing to bump into a friend of his and also a couple she'd met when they stayed at the castle a few months ago. This was one part of small-town life she found unexpectedly charming. Growing up in the massive suburban sprawl of Orlando, she'd never experienced anything like it.

And while she missed living near her parents and the rest of her family—missed it a *lot*—she liked pretty much everything about living in the Appalachians.

The next morning, she woke to the sun streaming in through the window and Jake's hand on her back, brushing her hair to the side so he could press open-mouthed kisses between her shoulder blades. She shivered as a smile spread across her face. "Ticklish."

"Always wake up to you halfway across the bed," he murmured between kisses.

"I move around a lot in my sleep." She rolled toward him, cupping his face to bring his lips to hers. While she loved the wild urgency that sometimes overcame them, these tender moments first thing in the morning were some of her favorite, something she'd rarely experienced. She'd never been much for spending the night with a man, preferring her own bed and the freedom to come and go as she pleased. With Jake, there was nowhere she'd rather be than right here in his arms.

They made love, rolling together across the bed in their tumble toward release. Afterward, Jake held her against his chest, something heavy in his expression. "I have to go out for a while after morning barn chores today."

She traced her fingers absently through the coarse hair on his chest. "Everything okay?"

"It's the anniversary of Alana's death." His arms tightened around her.

"Oh." She slid forward to press a kiss against his cheek. "I'm sorry."

"It's…well, it's not okay, exactly, but it'll be okay," he said in that frank way of his, the way he made everything sound manageable. "But I need to visit the cemetery, and then I need to go see her parents."

She swallowed. "Is…is there anything I can do?"

"Not today. I need to do this on my own. But another day, I'd really like to bring you to the cemetery with me."

"I'd like that too." She fought against the completely irrational twinge of hurt in her chest. Of course, he needed to do this alone. She was being weird and clingy. "Will I see you tonight, then?"

"At some point, yeah."

It was her morning to help with breakfast at the castle, so she dressed quickly. "Good luck today," she said with a kiss as they parted at the front door. "Call me if you need me."

"Thank you." He paused, taking her hand in his. "It makes it easier, knowing that you'll be here when I get home."

"I'm glad." She gave him a hug. "I love you."

"Love you too." He drew her in for one last kiss, and then he headed toward the barn while she took the path up to the castle.

She slipped in the side door that led directly into the kitchen.

"Good morning," Beatrice called over her shoulder as she rummaged in the refrigerator.

"Need help with anything?" Megan asked, grabbing a croissant off a pile on the island.

"Not a thing. Anthony and I have got it all under control." Anthony was a college student who helped Beatrice prepare breakfast for their guests before he headed to campus every morning. The kid was good in the kitchen and funny too.

"Got what under control?" he asked as he loped into the kitchen, apron tied around his waist and a net over his hair. "You mean that loaf of banana crunch bread I just took out of the oven?"

"Yum," Megan said with a smile.

"Hey, stranger!" Elle swept into the kitchen in a yellow sundress almost as bright as the smile on her face.

"You saw me yesterday," Megan protested.

"In passing," Elle said. "And don't even pretend you don't know what I mean. You've been spending every spare moment down at the farmhouse with Jake."

"Well, I live there now."

"You could at least pretend you still enjoy our company," Elle teased, still smiling widely. "But seriously, how are things?"

"Good," Megan said, feeling somewhat self-conscious at the revelation. She and Elle had known each other since they were about eight years old, and this was Megan's first serious relationship. It was a big deal, and they both knew it. "Really good."

"I'm so happy for you guys." Elle grabbed her in an impulsive hug.

"I feel like everything happened really fast to get us to this point," Megan said. "So now I'm looking forward to just slowing down and settling in, you know?"

Elle nodded. "I totally know. It was that way for Theo and me too. Until you get a chance to relax and settle, it all feels a bit surreal, right?"

"Exactly." Megan released a deep breath, glad Elle had put into words what she was feeling. "It's all really weird...but not weird."

Elle laughed. "I totally hear that. Do you guys want to join us here at the castle for dinner tonight? It's been a while."

"I'd love to, but today is the anniversary of his wife's death, so I think another day would be better."

Elle gave her a sympathetic look. "That must be really hard for him. And for you too, probably, knowing how to help him through it."

"Yeah, both," Megan said. "He's going to visit her grave and spend some time with her parents."

Elle sat next to Megan, and they ate croissants together before serving breakfast to their guests in the dining room. After a year in operation, the routine was comforting and familiar. Afterward, Megan went down the hall to their joint office to get her photography equipment for a scheduled portrait session with a young couple staying at the castle.

She met them out front. "Hi, I'm Megan."

"Carolyn," the woman told her. "And this is my husband,

Alex."

"Hi," Alex said, reaching out to shake Megan's hand. His gaze met hers briefly before darting away in that all-too-familiar way that made her cheeks heat and her fingers itch to shake her hair down over the scar. Would she ever get used to it?

"Nice to meet you both," she told them, turning to lead the way down the castle's front steps. "It's a beautiful day for photos. Before we get started, did you have any specific shots or locations in mind?"

She might not ever get used to people flinching at her appearance, but she could control her reaction to it. She could resist the urge to hide behind her hair, because this was still her face, dammit, and she wasn't ashamed of her scars. So, she held her head high as she led Carolyn and Alex through their portrait session. She didn't let the tears fall until she was locked safely in the bathroom after they'd left.

~

MEGAN WATCHED the timer on the oven, adjusting the temperature to make the lasagna cook as slowly as possible. She'd thought Jake would be home by now, thought she'd have a hot meal waiting for him, feed him and hold him and do what she could to make this day easier for him. But the lasagna had simmered so long the edges were starting to burn, so finally she pulled it out and left it to cool on the stovetop.

If he wasn't home soon, she'd put it in the fridge for tomorrow night. Why hadn't he at least called to check in? Maybe if he'd let her know what time to expect him, she wouldn't have an uneaten, overcooked lasagna sitting on the stove. She pressed a palm to her forehead. She was getting herself worked up over nothing. This was an emotional day for him. He was with Alana's parents. It's not like he was out with another woman.

But deep down, she wished she were with him. It would have been hard and maybe even awkward at times, but wasn't this what couples were supposed to do for each other? Be there for each other, even during the difficult times?

As the lasagna cooled in the kitchen, she sat on the couch and tried to read. Oreo and Cookie snuggled beside her while Barnaby sprawled on the floor by her feet. She was halfway through Jake's fourth book now and completely in love with the series. But tonight, she couldn't concentrate on Derrick and his crime-solving adventures. Instead, she found her attention migrating to the photo of Jake and Alana on the shelf by the window.

She'd seen it before, of course. It sat next to a photo of Jake with his mother and sister and one of him riding Twister that Megan herself had taken last month. Now, she stood and walked over, picking up the delicate silver frame. Alana beamed at her from behind the glass, so young, so innocent, so beautiful. She and Jake had their arms around each other, looking radiantly happy and in love.

Tears welled in Megan's eyes at the cruelty of it all, for everything Jake had been through and for Alana herself, thinking she had her whole life ahead of her with the man she loved, not knowing she would lose it all on her wedding day. Swiping at her eyes, Megan set the picture back on the shelf.

She picked up the photo of Jake on Twister, admiring his strong profile, his comfortable and commanding stance astride his horse. She'd taken it late one afternoon, with the sun's amber rays spilling over the treetops behind him, muting the other colors in the photo. She'd always liked to play with light —the sun in particular—in her photography, and this shot was one of her favorites.

The rest of the photos on the shelf were hers. There was a picture of her, Ruby, and Elle at Disney World a few years ago. Growing up in Orlando, they'd spent a lot of time at theme parks. Next to that was a photo of Megan with her parents in a blue glass frame, and a photo of Megan and her grandmother at Megan's high school graduation beside that.

There wasn't a photo of her and Jake. Somehow, she hadn't noticed that before. Why hadn't he added one? Why hadn't she?

Why wasn't he home yet?

She looked at the smiling, unscarred version of herself in the photos on the shelf, fingers going reflexively to her left cheek. Would she ever look that carefree again? Were she and Jake really building something solid here, or were they just playing house together while they both hid from the demons in their past?

She sat and tried to read for another hour, watching as the clock ticked past nine and kept going. Finally, she put the lasagna in the fridge, took the dogs out, and went to bed, alone.

By the time he got home that night, Jake was as emotionally drained as he'd been last year this time. He hadn't meant to stay out so late, but the day had gotten away from him. After he left the Robertson's, he'd stopped back by the cemetery on the way home. He'd needed to go alone, to sit there and vent the last of his grief by himself.

In truth, the day had hit him harder than he'd expected it to, and he was so incredibly glad he had Megan to hold him tonight. He'd spent so many unbearable nights alone in bed, aching for the touch, the company, the presence of another person. But when he let himself in through the front door of the farmhouse, he was greeted by silence.

The lights were out, and Megan was nowhere to be seen. He glanced at the clock, realizing it was past ten. That was still early for her to be in bed, but maybe she'd gotten bored by herself. Oreo and Cookie stirred in their crates, looking at Jake.

He should have called. It wasn't like him to get so caught up in his own business that he forgot to check in with her. But nothing about today had been ordinary. He walked down the hall, trying to soften his footsteps in case she was asleep. Sure enough, she was in bed, her back to the door, dark hair fanning across the pillow behind her.

Barnaby hopped up from his dog bed, walking over to Jake while his tail wagged in full loops. Jake bent to pet him. He undressed quietly and went into the bathroom to wash up before climbing in beside Megan. She rolled to face him, eyes glinting in the moonlight.

"How did it go?" she asked softly.

"It went. I'm just so glad to have you here tonight."

"Me too," she whispered.

He held on to her for a long time, and eventually they fell asleep like that, in each other's arms.

Over the next few days, things got back to normal, more or less. April rolled into May, and he was busy training Rumor and beginning Bug's early under saddle work. His new boarder was set to arrive at the end of the week. It had been two months now since he arrived at Rosemont Castle, and he felt comfortably established here, personally and professionally. Hopefully, things would continue to grow, on both fronts.

An idea had taken hold in his mind, a surprise for Megan that he thought might end up being just what she—and Bug— needed. When they were alone together, though, something still felt...off. He wasn't sure what it was or how to fix it, but she seemed distant at times in a way she never had before. Maybe he was imagining it. Or maybe he was even the cause of it. Maybe he was still adjusting to all the changes in his life, and she was just reacting to him.

On Tuesday night, they had dinner at the castle with Elle, Theo, and Ruby, sharing lots of laughter and good food. He and Megan walked back to the farmhouse afterward, hand in hand.

"Do you have photo albums?" she asked.

"What?" He had no idea where that question had come from.

"Pictures of you as a child, of you and Alana on your wedding day, anything. I've only ever seen those few photos you keep in the living room. You must have some, right?"

"I must," he agreed. "I do."

"Would you show them to me when we get home?"

"Yeah, of course."

"Thank you." She leaned in to give him a kiss.

Barnaby greeted them at the door when they entered the farmhouse, tail wagging enthusiastically. Jake leashed him while Megan went into the living room to get Oreo and Cookie out of their crates so they could walk all the dogs together.

"I can really see how a fenced-in yard comes in handy," Megan commented as they circled around behind the barn. "You can just open the back door and let them out."

"That would be nice," he agreed. They looped around the grounds and back to the house. "I have a few boxes in the office I haven't gotten around to unpacking yet. I'm pretty sure one of them has photos in it."

"Let's go dig through them," Megan said with a gentle smile. "I want to see young Jake."

"There may not be many," he cautioned. "My mom wasn't really the photo album type."

"I'm sorry." She rested a hand on his biceps as they walked down the hall to the office together. "I've never really been in here," she commented as she stood in the doorway, surveying the room. "That's quite a bookshelf."

He looked over at the built-in shelving he'd had installed after he moved in. The shelves extended from floor to ceiling along the back wall, and he'd already filled them with books. "It doesn't compare to Theo's library, but I've always wanted one of my own. Books have always been my escape."

"Theo's library is almost overwhelming, it's so impressive," Megan commented as she walked over to survey the shelves. "This is more personal and inviting. Have you read them all?"

"Almost all." He walked to the closet and pulled out a box. "Okay, let's find some pictures." He pulled it open and sifted through various papers and odds and ends inside until he got to the framed photos beneath. There was one of him and his sister on the beach when he was about seven and she was ten, and one of them with their mom.

"Do you keep in touch with your sister?" Megan asked as she looked at the photos. "You never talk about her."

"We call each other on birthdays and holidays. I see her once or twice a year. There's no bad blood. We just…aren't close, I guess. She moved away after Mom died and created a new life for herself."

"That's sad," Megan murmured. "I'm an only child, but I always wished for a sibling when I was little. I made up for it with friends." She smiled to herself.

"Elle and Ruby?"

"Yeah. Lifelong BFFs."

He rummaged deeper in the box until he found his wedding album. He'd never had any of their wedding photos framed. The entire event was such a dichotomy of emotions, the over-whelming love and excitement he'd felt as they exchanged vows, the terror when Alana had fallen. He hadn't fully grasped the severity of things until the next day, when Alana was still comatose and the doctors started talking about living wills.

He wouldn't even have this album if Tina hadn't made it for him. She'd given it to him on his and Alana's first wedding anniversary, a bittersweet gift. That familiar heaviness spread around his chest as he handed it to Megan.

She squeezed his hand as she sat cross-legged on the floor and started going through the photos. "She was so beautiful in her wedding dress," she whispered.

"She was perfect," he said quietly, looking down at the photo of him and Alana exchanging vows at the front of the church. Alana's blonde hair had been tied back in a sleek knot and covered with a long veil. Health and happiness sparkled in her blue eyes, so much life there, all of which would be snuffed out a few hours later. Her heart kept beating for another nine years, but he would never see her beautiful blue eyes again, never hear her laugh or see her smile, never carry her over the threshold into their home.

"We took all our wedding portraits before her fall, so her mom went ahead and put the album together for me afterward. We cut the cake, had our first dance. She went outside with a couple of her friends to get some fresh air, and...didn't come back."

"So awful," she murmured.

"It was."

"Thanks for sharing her with me." Megan rested a hand on his leg and put the album back in the box. As she climbed to her feet, there was something in her eyes Jake hadn't seen there in a long time...not since she used to comb her hair over the side of her face to hide her scar.

They watched TV and went to bed together like they always did, but something was different, something had changed. Megan was distant. She almost seemed...hurt. But why? By the time he woke beside her the next morning, he'd convinced himself it was just a weird reaction to seeing photos of his wedding to Alana. But when he tried to kiss her and she rolled away, he knew it was something more.

"What's going on?" he asked.

She kept her back to him. "I just..."

"Tell me." Because she was starting to scare him.

"I don't know how to say this without sounding like a bitch, but you're still in love with your wife."

"What?" He sat up, blinking the sleep from his eyes. "I mean, of course I'll always love her in some way, but it has nothing to do with the love I feel for you."

Megan rolled to face him, tears shimmering in her eyes. "Last night, you said she was perfect, and you know what? You're right. She *was* perfect. How could I ever compete with that?" She pressed a hand against the scarred side of her face. "Maybe it's what drew us to each other in the first place—all this fucking tragedy—or maybe you're only attracted to me because you feel sorry for me, or—"

"I'm going to stop you right there." His stomach had gone sour. "There's nothing tragic about you, Megan, and as for your scars, I don't even think about them. Do you realize how many scars I have from a lifetime spent working with horses? You think I care about an imperfection in your skin?"

She turned away. "I don't know what to think."

An uncomfortable heat spread across his skin. "I think you're being ridiculous right now."

"Am I?" She sat up to face him. "Because half the town can barely stand to look at me. Are you sure you're not with me because I take the attention off *you*?"

"Well that's pretty fucking insulting." He stared at her for a long minute as anger warred with hurt inside him.

She slid out of bed and started pulling on clothes. "I should go."

"The hell you should." He strode to his dresser and pulled on a fresh pair of boxers. Barnaby watched from his dog bed, ears pinned at the harsh words being exchanged. "Obviously, we have some things to talk about."

"I just...I think maybe we jumped into this too quickly," she said quietly.

"Well, we're here now, and I don't think I'm the one having trouble with it. Maybe you need to take a harder look at yourself, Megan." They faced each other across the bedroom.

Her cheeks were pink, her eyes wide and glossy. "So, that's how you want to play this? Pin it on me?"

"You know what, maybe we do need some time apart." He pulled on jeans and a T-shirt. "Let me know when you're ready to talk about what's really going on here."

And with that, he stormed out of the bedroom, out of the house, not slowing until he'd reached the barn.

## 17

By midmorning, Jake had dropped a fifty-pound bag of grain on his foot and soaked himself with the water hose. Obviously, his mind was elsewhere. He wasn't sure which was worse, the realization of how insecure Megan still was about her scars or the hurtful things she'd said. And now he wasn't sure what to do about it. He'd said they needed some time apart, but probably what they needed more was to talk, *really* talk, once they'd both calmed down and cooled off.

He spent the morning in the barn before heading out to training sessions with two of his offsite clients. By the time he made it back to the farmhouse, it was almost dinnertime. As soon as he walked through the front door, he could tell it was too quiet inside. Barnaby greeted him at the door, but there were no rustling noises from the foster dogs in their crates. Megan didn't usually take them to work at the castle with her, but today, they were gone.

*She* was gone. And as much as he'd hoped she would be here waiting for him, ready to apologize and talk things through, he wasn't exactly surprised she wasn't. She'd probably gone up to the castle for the night to give them both some space.

Maybe that was what they needed. But first, he wanted to

see her, to see what exactly had happened that morning. And so, he turned around and left the farmhouse, striding toward the castle. He pushed through its heavy wooden doors, poking his head into various rooms until he found Ruby in the study with her laptop. She looked up, an apologetic expression on her face.

"Is she here?" he asked.

Her lips twisted. "She booked a flight to stay with her parents for a little while."

He rocked back on his heels. She'd gone all the way to Florida? *What the hell, Megan?* "Did she tell you why?"

Ruby looked down at her hands. "Yes."

"So, she's gone."

"She'll be back." Ruby looked up with sad eyes. "I just think...I think she's more upset about her scars than any of us realized."

Megan would come back to the castle. But would she come back to him? And would they be able to work things out if she did?

～

MEGAN HAD EXPECTED a lot more sympathy when she arrived at her parents' Orlando doorstep that Wednesday afternoon. Sure, there had been plenty of hugs and tears when she first saw them, but now she was getting the not-so-subtle impression her mom thought she'd made a huge mistake running out on Jake the way she had.

"I'm sorry it's not for happier reasons, but you know we're always thrilled to have you home for a visit," her mom said, pulling her in for a hug.

"It feels good to be here." Megan followed her into the kitchen to help her fix supper. She'd gotten so caught up in everything with Jake that she hadn't talked to her mom as much as usual this month. And she regretted that now. She'd always been so close with her parents. It wasn't like her to blow them off for a guy. A lot of things she'd done lately weren't like her.

"You want to talk about it?" her mom asked as she placed a cutting board and vegetables in front of Megan so she could start making the salad.

"No...yes...I don't know." She blew out a breath and stabbed the knife into a red bell pepper.

"Careful," her mom said with a chuckle. "Can I tell you what I think?"

"Could I stop you even if I wanted to?" Megan felt a smile tugging at the corners of her lips.

"No, and you wouldn't have come running home like this if you didn't want my advice, so here it comes." Her mom mixed ingredients for a marinade in a large Ziploc bag as she spoke. "The first thing we need to talk about is your scars."

"What about them?" She resisted the urge to touch her face, because then she'd have to wash her hands again before she finished chopping vegetables.

"It broke my heart when we brought you home after your accident last year." Her mom's tone softened. "I'd never seen you look so sad or...broken. And I'm not talking about your face—or your arm—for that matter. I mean your spirit."

"Mom..." Her voice cracked.

"No, you're going to hear me out." Her mom squeezed a lemon into the bag and gave it a shake. "You've always been outgoing and flirtatious. Men are drawn to you, and it's not just because of your looks. But yes, you're gorgeous, Megan. You know we fielded modeling offers for you in high school. But that's not why the boys flocked to you, or it's not the only reason, anyway. It's you. It's your bubbly personality and your infectious laugh. You're smart, and you're caring, and you're fun to be around."

"Mom..."

"I'm not finished yet." Her mom pointed a carrot in her

direction before plopping it on the cutting board. "My point is that something inside you changed after your accident, like a light went out. I saw it. Your father saw it. Your friends saw it."

"How do you know that?" she asked, fighting past the tightness in her throat.

"Because Elle called me, last winter. She was worried about you. We all were. It wasn't like you to stop dating, or to start spending more time behind your camera than in front of it."

"I was trying to launch my photography career," she protested.

"Yes, but it was more than that, and you know it as well as I do. How many selfies have you taken this year? How many of them did you post on social media?" She paused for a moment with her eyebrows raised, and Megan dropped her gaze to the cutting board.

"Not many."

"You're hiding, and from what, Meg? Have you looked at yourself in the mirror lately, I mean, *really* looked?"

"I see myself every day." She felt the hot press of tears and behind it, a blinding surge of anger. "Those scars will always be there, and now they're the first thing people notice when they meet me. They cringe, Mom, like they can't bear to look at me."

"Oh, sweetheart." Her mom took the knife from Megan's hands and pulled her in for another hug. "I'm sorry, so sorry."

Megan straightened, wiping the tears from her face with the back of her hand before she resumed cutting vegetables.

"How often does that actually happen?" her mom asked. "Because although I want to bitch-slap anyone who would ever cringe at the sight of my beautiful baby girl, I think maybe your scars are more noticeable to you than they are to anyone else."

"It happens." Megan thought of the man from her portrait session last week. "Not as often as it used to, but it still happens."

Her mom pulled out her cell phone. "Smile." She lifted the phone and snapped a photo, then turned it around to show

Megan. "Fluorescent lights are unforgiving. We all look like crap in front of the bathroom mirror. But look at yourself the way I see you, Meg. Unless the sun hits it just so, I hardly notice it."

Megan looked at the photo on her mom's phone. She'd shied away from photos of herself this year, afraid of what she would see. And what she saw now was a tired, glum version of herself with barely-visible scarring along the left side of her face. "It's too dark in your kitchen to really see them."

Her mom rested a hand on Megan's arm. "I hate more than anything in the world that you have to live with these scars. It's horribly unfair, and if I could do anything to change it for you, I would. I've cried and cried since your accident. Your father and I both have."

Megan looked away, her vision blurring behind a sheen of tears.

"But the thing I hate most is the way it's changed you inside."

"Mom..." she whispered.

"Now, tell me about what happened with Jake."

"I just..." She took a deep breath, trying to make sense of the emotions churning in her chest. "His wife was perfect, Mom. Jake even said so himself. She was just this beautiful, sweet, perfect person, and they loved each other so much. How can I ever compete with that?"

"Oh, sweetie, it's not a competition."

"I know." She looked down at the pile of half-chopped vegetables in front of her. "But, if I'm comparing myself to Alana, surely he is too. What if I'm just a way out of his loneliness and grief? What if we're just helping each other hide from our scars?"

"Has he ever given you any reason to think he's comparing you to his wife, or that he finds you anything less than perfect too?"

"No," she whispered, staring at the carrot her mom had put on the cutting board.

"Is it possible that this is all in your head? That maybe you overreacted based on your own insecurities and pushed him away because you got scared?"

"Maybe," Megan conceded after she'd stared at the carrot so long it had turned into an orange blur before her eyes. "Probably."

"Then as much as I love having you here, you need to go back to Virginia and sort this out. Because you and Jake love each other, and that's not something you walk away from without making sure you've done everything you can to try to save it."

"But what if I can't get past this, Mom?" Hot tears rolled down her cheeks. "I don't know how to be the woman he deserves."

"Well, that part's easy. Just be yourself. Be honest with him, let him help you, let him love you, just like you've done for him."

## 18

*M*egan took a deep breath to steady herself as she asked the driver to drop her off at the farmhouse instead of going up to the main castle. She could have used Elle and Ruby for moral support, but she needed to do this on her own. Hopefully, Jake would be willing to hear her out. Because after two days in Florida under constant helpings of her mom's tough love and advice, Megan was ready to own her mistakes, if Jake would give her the chance.

The farmhouse was empty, though, except for Barnaby, who bounced and wagged his pleasure to see her.

"I missed you too, buddy." She knelt and pulled him into her arms for a hug. As she stood, she noticed a picture frame on the counter. That hadn't been there before she left. She was positive. She walked over and picked it up, and her heart somersaulted into her throat when she saw the selfie she'd taken at the top of the Ferris wheel at the Spring Fling. She and Jake were facing each other, kissing, as she'd held her phone overhead.

Her scar was turned toward the camera, glistening slightly in the sunlight, and yet, it was hard to see past the radiant looks on their faces, the joy that glimmered in the air between them, and the vibrant colors of the fairgrounds below.

"I'm an idiot." She carried the photo to the shelf by the window and nestled it right in the middle of the individual photos of her and Jake. Then, she left the house, walking to the barn. She'd expected to find him working with one of the horses, but nothing prepared her for what she saw as she rounded the barn to face the outdoor ring. Her breath caught in her throat.

Jake was riding Bug.

"Oh my God," she gasped.

Jake turned, straightening in the saddle as he caught sight of her. He reached down to give Bug a reassuring rub. "Megan."

"I'm back. I'm…you're riding Bug. I'm sorry, I just…"

"It turns out she's either a really quick learner or she'd already had more training than we thought," Jake said as he dismounted, leading Bug in her direction.

"When I called Elle yesterday, she said Bug had an adoption pending. I wasn't…I wasn't sure I'd even get to see her again."

"I adopted her," Jake said. "It was going to be a surprise for you, since you two were so bonded. I thought maybe we could trail ride together, you on Bug and me on Twister. And then…" His jaw clenched.

"I'm so sorry," she whispered, tears swimming across her vision. "I, um…I'm a total asshole for treating you the way I did the other morning, for everything I said."

"Yeah, you were," he said, but his expression had softened.

"Apparently, I have some issues from my accident that I need to work through, which my mom laid out for me pretty hardcore while I was in Orlando."

"Did she?" He smiled, just slightly, his eyes locked on hers.

"Yeah, like the fact that I'm more hung up on my scars than anyone else is, least of all you, who's never given me any reason to doubt you, and yet, I panicked and ran the first time we had an argument…which was all my fault, by the way." She blew out a deep breath, stepping forward to stroke Bug's face. "And I'm just so sorry, because I love you so much, and I hope I haven't ruined everything."

Then Jake's hands were on her waist, drawing her in for a kiss. His lips closed over hers, hot and urgent, filling her with warmth from head to toe. "Stop apologizing and kiss me."

"But…" She was kissing him, and tears were streaming over her cheeks, and Bug's mane was in her face, and she was so happy she could hardly think straight.

"We've both got scars, Megan, inside and out. We've been through a lot, and we're going to make mistakes. We're going to hurt each other. But as long as we're willing to work at it and learn from our mistakes, we'll be just fine, don't you think?"

"I hope so," she whispered through her tears.

"Life's short, and true love like what we have is rare. I don't want to let it go to waste, do you?"

"No." She pressed her forehead against his, breathing him in, his masculine scent mixed with the horse beside them and the earth beneath their feet. It all felt like home.

Jake cupped her scarred cheek with his right hand, his brown eyes boring into hers. "I love you, Megan. We've started something wonderful here together, and I can't wait to see where it takes us. And now we've got Bug to round out the four-legged family."

The horse stomped a hoof, nuzzling her nose through the loose strands of Megan's hair. Her brown eyes were bright and curious, no trace of the fear and distrust she'd displayed when she first arrived at Rosemont Castle.

"I can't believe you adopted her." Megan's voice had dropped to a whisper again.

"You two were meant to be together, just like you and I are. Plus, she and Twister have really hit it off since I started turning them out together. I think it means we're all meant to stay together, don't you?"

"Yeah." She stared into the eyes of the man she loved, and everything that had been out of sorts inside her since her accident, everything in her that had ever felt restless or unsettled, seemed to calm as her world snapped into perfect alignment. "I do."

# DEAR READER

I hope you enjoyed *Once Upon a Cowboy*! We saw Elle and Theo fall in love in *If the Shoe Fits* (Almost Royal #1), and now Megan has gotten her happily ever with Jake. So, as you may have guessed, it's Ruby's turn next. *Let Your Hair Down* (Almost Royal #3) is Ruby's book, and it's a fun one! (Hint: #RubyGoes-Rogue) The first chapter is included as a bonus at the end of this book.

Sign up for my newsletter for exclusive news and giveaways and receive a free copy of my award-winning novella, *Only You,* just for subscribing. If you enjoy chatting about books, I'd love for you to join my reader group on Facebook. It's a great place for us to stay in touch, and I often ask for help naming upcoming characters and pets plus lots of other fun reader group exclusives.

Hope to see you there!
Rachel Lacey

# ACKNOWLEDGMENTS

Thank you so much to my agent, Sarah Younger, and the rest of the NYLA team for all your help with *Once Upon a Cowboy*. I'm also hugely grateful to Sarah and my awesome sister Juliana for your horse expertise. Any mistakes are my own!

Thank you to my always amazing critique partner, Annie Rains, for your invaluable advice and for titling this book for me!

A special thank you to my loyal reader Marsha McDaniel for letting me use her real-life horse, Twister, as the inspiration for Jake's horse in *Once Upon a Cowboy* and to Donamae Kutska for inspiring rescue horse Dusty Star. Rescue horse Bug as well as Megan's rescue dogs are all inspired by real-life animals at local shelters who've all gone on to find their forever homes (both in real life and on the page!)

A huge thank you to all the readers, bloggers, and reviewers who've read my books and supported me along the way. Love you all!

xoxo
Rachel

## ALSO BY RACHEL LACEY

**Rock Star Duet**

*Unwritten*

*Encore*

**The Stranded Series**

*Crash and Burn*

*Lost in Paradise*

**The Risking It All Series**

*Rock with You*

*Run to You*

*Crazy for You*

*Can't Forget You*

*My Gift is You*

**The Love to the Rescue Series**

*Unleashed*

*For Keeps*

*Ever After*

*Only You*

**The Almost Royal Series**

*If the Shoe Fits*

*Once Upon a Cowboy*

*Let Your Hair Down*

# LET YOUR HAIR DOWN EXCERPT

## Chapter 1

Ruby Keller crept past a row of ornate marble statues into the gardens beyond. Her heels clicked against stone pavers as she followed a path leading away from the Langdon family estate. Behind her, the wedding reception was in full swing, music and laughter drifting on the air, as rich as the scent of the rose-bushes blooming on either side of the path.

She wasn't running away from her best friend's wedding. On the contrary, Elle and Theo's wedding was by far the most beautiful and amazing event she'd ever attended, held at this beautiful estate just outside London, but there were drawbacks to being here without a date. Ruby was accustomed to flying solo at events. It usually didn't faze her. But usually she had her best friends by her side. Now, Elle was married, and Megan was here with her boyfriend, Jake, and they were adorably, disgustingly in love.

For the last half hour, Ruby had fought off the advances of an obnoxiously drunk man named Lester who couldn't seem to take a hint, not even when she'd pointedly turned to her cell phone and begun scrolling through her social media while he droned on about his accomplishments in the field of financial investment. So, when he went to the bar for another drink, Ruby decided to make herself scarce.

She was officially peopled out for the night and hoping to find some peace and quiet here in the gardens. Just for a little while. Then, she'd be a good Maid of Honor and go back inside to join the party. But, honestly, events like this were exhausting for an introvert.

"Ruby? Are you out here?"

Lester's deep voice echoed through the garden. It was a shame he was such an ass because he had a sexy voice, and she'd always had a thing for British accents. He wasn't hard to look at either. But he was obnoxious to the point it bordered on harassment. She'd already told him she wasn't interested—several times—and yet, here he was. She stepped off the stone path, walking between two rows of rosebushes.

"I saw you come out here and thought you might like company," he called.

*You thought wrong, buddy.*

She extended her middle finger in his general direction as she ducked behind a rosebush, bending awkwardly in her floor-length satin dress. There was a sharp tug at her hair, and she reared back with a gasp, right hand raised reflexively in case she needed to defend herself, but no one was there. She was alone, deep in the garden away from the lighted path, her hair snagged on a rosebush.

Well, this was embarrassing. She tipped her head forward, attempting to tug free, but to no avail. Her glasses slid off her nose and tumbled into the darkness. Ruby exhaled in frustration as she reached behind her head, pricking her finger on a thorn in the process.

"For crying out loud," she muttered. Her fingers encountered more thorns...and more hair. Her meticulously constructed up-do—for which she'd spent hours at the salon that morning with the rest of the bridal party—was now engaged in a tug-of-war with the rosebush. And her hair seemed to be losing.

"You look like you could use a hand," a man said from behind her.

She tensed, half-blind without her glasses and unable to turn around, stuck in a ridiculous crouch lest she rip her hair out by the roots. But this voice—while still deep, masculine, and British—was different. Softer. Kinder. Not Lester. And she really could use a hand.

"You could say that," she said.

"Hold still," the man said, and a moment later, she felt a gentle tug at the back of her head and fingers poking through her hair. "Let me know if I'm hurting you. It's tangled pretty badly back here."

"It's fine," she said, wincing slightly. "Do what you need to do."

"Almost got it," he said.

Ruby rested her palms on her thighs, attempting to balance in her awkward position. Her rescuer had a nice voice, rich and soothing. He sounded young, and yeah, she was still digging the British accent.

"You're free," he announced.

"Thank you," she breathed, straightening to her full height. One hand went automatically into her hair, which felt like a disheveled mess. The man in front of her was tall and slim, with dark hair and wearing a black tux, like nearly every other man in attendance tonight. That was about all she could tell without her glasses. "I really appreciate it."

"Happy to help," he said, extending a hand in her direction. "Flynn Bowen."

She took it and shook, impressed by the strength of his grasp. "Ruby Keller."

"A pleasure to meet you, Ruby." He leaned forward, his voice dropping conspiratorially. "So, who are you hiding from out here?"

"Excuse me?" She crouched, feeling around for her glasses. Her fingers closed over them, and she slipped them onto her face, standing to face Flynn. And *whoa*. She blinked, attempting to school her expression, because he was hot...in an adorable sort of way. His dark hair was slightly longer than seemed to be the acceptable "dress code" for the other men here tonight. An unruly lock had fallen over his forehead. His eyes were crinkled in a friendly smile, sparkling with humor.

"See, I was already out here...also hiding," he said with a wink. "My entire family is in there. The Bowens are longtime friends of the Langdons. My parents, brother, sisters, and all their spouses are here tonight. I'm the youngest of five," he explained. "And the only single one. My mother won't stop trying to introduce me to every available woman in the ballroom, so I came out to wander the gardens. And then I saw you sneaking off into the bushes."

"I guess I'm out here for similar reasons," she told him as she attempted to smooth over what remained of her hairdo. "No family here, though, but I'm the only single one left in my group of friends. I'm surprised your mother didn't already introduce us."

"I expect she would have if she knew you," Flynn said, his easy smile never faltering. "But alas, you're American, so I think she would consider you a lost cause."

"She doesn't want you to date an American?" Ruby asked.

"Oh, nothing like that. It's just, I imagine you're only here for the wedding and will be flying home soon after. My mother isn't exactly trying to find me a one-night stand." His grin widened.

Ruby laughed. Flynn's exuberance was infectious. "Well, she'd be right, I guess. I'm sticking around for a week or so to do some sightseeing, but then I'll be flying back to Virginia."

"Really?" Flynn gestured for her to follow him toward a bench on the main path. "What areas are you going to visit?"

"That's the thing." Her body buzzed with a mixture of

excitement and nerves. "I haven't made any plans. I'm going to just...see what happens."

"How intriguing." Flynn's eyebrows rose. "A woman with a sense of adventure. I like that."

"If you only knew." She shook her head, feeling what remained of her bun sliding around loosely. "This is so unlike me. I'm an over-planner. I have a spreadsheet for...well, everything."

"Define everything," Flynn said, his gaze locked on hers, intense, but not in an alarming way, more like he was hanging on her every word.

"I have a spreadsheet to help me manage all my spreadsheets."

Flynn laughed, resting a hand on her shoulder. "That is unusual, I'll admit."

She grinned. "I'm an unusual woman, what can I say?"

"I like it. Tell me more." He sat on the bench, patting the empty spot beside him.

She sat, feeling a hundred times lighter than she had a few minutes ago. "Do you want the short version or the long version?"

"Ruby, there you are!" Lester came around a bend in the path, beelining toward her. He stopped in front of the bench with a slight frown. "Who are you?"

"Flynn Bowen," Flynn said. "And you are?"

"Lester Mayberry," he announced with an air of self-importance. "Ruby and I were just about to dance. Weren't we, Ruby?"

"Actually, you asked, and I said I wasn't in the mood," she told him, letting her voice fall flat in annoyance.

"Well, I..." Lester gaped, seemingly—*finally*—at a loss for words. "What happened to your hair?"

"I decided to take it down," she said, reaching up to tug out a bobby pin. "What do you think?"

Lester stared at her, his mouth opening and closing in silent confusion.

"I think Ruby's hair looks rather lovely this way," Flynn said. "Don't you?"

"Yes, of course," Lester stammered.

"Well, nice meeting you," Flynn said pointedly.

"Likewise, I'm sure," Lester muttered before turning and walking off in the direction of the estate.

"Is that wanker the reason you were hiding behind a rose-bush when I found you?" Flynn asked, his tone a mixture of humor and annoyance.

"Yes. Does my hair look that terrible?"

"Not at all." Flynn gave her a discerning look. "Although it does look a bit like you and I were going at it behind that rosebush."

"Now who's a wanker?" she teased, ridiculously charmed by his accent.

"Guilty as charged."

"My hair's a total mess. I can tell." She patted the back of her head, coming out with another bobby pin…and a thorn. "I'm going to take it down."

"I'll help if you like," he offered, reaching over to tug another pin out of her hair. And since there were about a million more where that came from, she agreed.

"Thank you."

"So, to answer your question before we were so rudely interrupted, I'd like the long version."

"What?" She set a bobby pin in the growing pile on the bench between them.

"You were about to tell me the story behind your adventure here in London and why you've always played it safe before."

"Oh, that." She glanced over at Flynn. "The long version, huh?"

"I think we have time for it while we pull out all these pins." He held one up for emphasis.

"I have primary immunodeficiency," she told him. "I couldn't be around other kids much when I was growing up, because of my faulty immune system, and even so, I was sick a lot. My mom homeschooled me for most of my childhood."

"That must have been very difficult for you." Flynn set a pin on the pile and reached over to give her hand a squeeze.

"I received a bone marrow transplant from my sister when I was seventeen, and I've been mostly as good as new since, although I still have to be careful. But the point of the story is that I spent my childhood locked away safe and bored in my bedroom. I guess it made me cautious. I tend to overanalyze things to death before making a decision, and, you know…the spreadsheets."

"Lots of spreadsheets," Flynn repeated with a nod.

"I'm that person who takes her laptop with her everywhere she goes."

"I see you left it behind tonight," he commented with a smile.

"I left it at home." She sucked in a deep breath and blew it out. "I've never traveled before. This is my first time outside of the United States, and I'm ready to have the adventure of a lifetime, all by myself, no laptop to hide behind."

Flynn tugged another pin out of her hair, his gaze catching hers in the muted light of the garden. "That is one of the most fascinating and brave stories I've ever heard."

"It's not," she protested. A section of her hair tumbled down her back as she removed another pin. "I'm just taking a vacation. Millions of people do it every day."

"Not like this." He pointed a finger at her. "You said it yourself, this is going to be the adventure of a lifetime."

"Well, I hope it will be. Honestly, it's pretty intimidating now that I'm here. I mean, I've been so caught up in wedding activities, I haven't really had a chance to think about what I'll do tomorrow when it's all over."

"Hence the adventure."

"Yes. I've got a hotel booked in London for the next few nights, but beyond that…who knows?"

"Would you like a few suggestions?" he asked.

"I'd love some, actually."

"I assume you know all the main tourist attractions, but do you enjoy theater? The West End is, in my opinion, superior even to Broadway. You can find anything you're interested in, musical, comedy, opera."

"Theater." Ruby felt a flutter of joy in her chest. "I've never been to a Broadway show. In fact, the only theater I've ever seen were the plays Elle was in back in high school."

"Elle who just married Theo?" Flynn's eyebrow went up.

"The very one. She considered being an actress after high school, although that obviously didn't work out. But yeah, I think I'd love to go to the theater." Her hair tumbled loose over her shoulders, and while she usually didn't like it, tonight it didn't feel half bad, shielding her from the cool September breeze.

"The National Gallery has some amazing artwork, da Vinci, Rembrandt. And you absolutely must visit Hampstead Heath. It has the most amazing views. Then there's Oxford Street if you enjoy shopping, and Camden Market has just about every cuisine you could imagine."

"Wow," she breathed, completely taken with every idea he'd just put in her head.

"You mentioned that you wanted to take this adventure on your own, but if you're interested in a tour guide, I'd be happy to show you around London tomorrow."

"Oh, I don't know…" She liked Flynn a lot, but she'd planned to do this on her own. And honestly, they'd just met. She didn't know a thing about him. It would be crazy to let him be her tour guide tomorrow. Then again, wasn't the point of this trip go to with the flow, to abandon her plans? But still, this felt like a pretty big leap. "Let me get back to you on that."

Flynn Bowen couldn't remember ever feeling so enchanted by someone he'd just met. He tugged another pin out of Ruby's hair, watching as it spilled in a dark waterfall down her back. And he found himself irrationally hoping she would take him up on his offer.

She stared at him from behind black-rimmed glasses, her pretty pink lips pursed in thought. "Not sure it's wise to let a total stranger show me around London, although it *would* be adventurous."

"You and I are strangers, but we have a mutual friend," he told her. "Theo and I have known each other our whole lives. We attended the same primary and secondary school, although I was a few years behind him."

"So, the Earl of Highcastle will vouch for your character. That's what you're telling me?" She gave him another one of those grins that made her eyes crinkle at the corners.

"Essentially, yes," he told her with a smile of his own.

"You don't have anything else to do tomorrow?" she asked.

"Not tomorrow, as it's Sunday, but I do have business in Wales on Monday."

"Tell me more about yourself, Flynn. What do you do for a living?"

He leaned back, staring into the fountain in front of them. "A better question might be, what *don't* I do?"

"I...don't know what that means."

"It means I've tried a number of positions within the family business, but none seem to have been the right fit." He watched the water as it splashed into the basin of the fountain, only to be sucked back up through the plumbing and begin its journey all over again. That was how he felt most of the time. One of these days, he would find the right position within the company, the one that would launch him right over the edge and out of this holding pattern.

In the meantime, he needed to dedicate himself one hundred percent to his upcoming assignment in Dubai. His parents had taken a chance on him, allowing him to oversee the construction of what would become one of Exeter Hotels' largest locations, and he couldn't let them down.

"I think that happens to a lot of us." Ruby set the last pin on the bench between them and ran her fingers through her hair, smoothing out the bumps and waves. "In fact, Elle, Megan, and I had all been bouncing between jobs until we won that magazine contest last year."

"You won a magazine contest?"

She nodded. "To manage Rosemont Castle. It's how we met Theo." She gestured toward the estate, where Theo was inside dancing with his new bride.

"Ah."

"Does it look okay?" she asked, tugging at a strand of her hair.

"You look beautiful." He studied her with a smile. "I didn't get a good look at you before your run-in with the rosebush, but I think I might prefer it down."

"Really? I never wear it down."

"No? That's a shame. You have lovely hair."

"I can't stand when it gets in my face."

"May I?" He picked up a pin and gestured to her hair.

"You want to do my hair for me?" she asked, amusement and surprise mixing in her tone.

"I have three sisters." He lifted the hair away from the left side of her face and secured it with several pins, then did the same on the other side.

"Three sisters?"

"I told you I'm the youngest of five. There." He sat back and surveyed his work. "Not bad, if I do say so myself."

Ruby reached up to touch her new hairdo. "I think I like it. I might change my mind when I see myself in a mirror, though."

He lifted his hands in front of him. "I'll take no offense if you hate it. Shall we go find a mirror, then?"

"I suppose I've hidden out here in the gardens long enough." She stood, smoothing her hands over the front of her dress. "It's been nice chatting with you, though."

"Do you really not want to dance, or did you just not want to dance with Lester?" he asked, holding out his elbow.

She slipped her hand through it with a small smile. "So polite. I'm not much of a dancer, I'm afraid, but my objection was mainly to dancing with Lester."

"In that case, after you freshen up, would you care to dance?" He gave her his most charming smile.

"I'd love to." Her eyes twinkled in the moonlight.

"Excellent." They walked into the ballroom, arm-in-arm. The band played a lively tune at one end of the room, and the dancefloor was packed. At the center, he could see the bride and groom. He nodded toward them. "They look like they're having a good time."

"They sure do." Ruby's face lit with a smile, and Flynn's breath caught in his throat. "What?" she asked.

"I just got my first look at you in actual light, and I had no idea I'd been sitting outside with the prettiest woman at the party." He nudged her shoulder playfully. Ruby scoffed at his compliment, but he wasn't joking, not this time. She was lovely, with her dark hair cascading over her shoulders, pinned back to accent her heart-shaped face and those rich chocolate eyes shining behind her glasses. Ruby wore a floor-length pink dress—a bridesmaid's dress—and it hugged her petite frame just right.

"I'm going to the ladies' room. I'll be right back."

"I'll be waiting." He turned toward the bar, only to see his mother waving him over.

"Flynn," she called. "There you are."

And he felt a bit like Ruby had in the garden when Lester Mayberry caught up with them, because there was a woman standing beside his mother, a blonde in a knee-length black dress smiling shyly in his direction.

"Darling, this is Polly Creekmore," his mother said. "Polly, this is my son, Flynn."

He glanced over his shoulder in the direction Ruby had gone. This time, it would be her turn to save him.

# ABOUT THE AUTHOR

 Rachel Lacey is a contemporary romance author and semi-reformed travel junkie. She's been climbed by a monkey on a mountain in Japan, gone scuba diving on the Great Barrier Reef, and camped out overnight in New York City for a chance to be an extra in a movie. These days, the majority of her adventures take place on the pages of the books she writes. She lives in warm and sunny North Carolina with her husband, son, and a variety of rescue pets.

facebook.com/RachelLaceyAuthor

twitter.com/rachelslacey

instagram.com/rachelslacey

amazon.com/author/rachellacey

bookbub.com/authors/rachel-lacey

CPSIA information can be obtained
at www.ICGtesting.com
Printed in the USA
LVHW111514121219
640280LV00003B/413/P